Nightshades

ALSO BY MELISSA F. OLSON

NIGHTSHADES

MELISSA F. OLSON

A TOM DOHERTY ASSOCIATES BOOK

NEW YORK

NIGHTSHADES

Cover design by Fort

Edited by Lee Harris

A Tor.com Book
Published by Tom Doherty Associates, LLC
175 Fifth Avenue
New York, NY 10010

www.tor.com

Tor® is a registered trademark of Tom Doherty Associates, LLC.

ISBN 978-0-7653-8849-0 (ebook)
ISBN 978-0-7653-8850-6 (trade paperback)

First Edition: July 2016

For all the nerds who like the same weird stuff I do.
You guys are why I'm here.

The revelation that plain old homo sapiens are not the planet's only sentient species came not with a bang or a whimper, but with mocking disbelief and millions of *Dracula*-themed memes reigning over Facebook. It took time—and many, many independent confirmations of Subject A's otherworldly physiology—before the public could eventually be convinced, one by one, that yes, the bloodsuckers were real, and they were among us. In this way, the sudden knowledge managed to creep over us, like a celebrity death hoax or the news of a natural disaster on the far side of the planet. By the time most of the world's population had become cognizant of the new world order, they'd already had time to observe that life went on as it had before. Yes, vampires were real—and no one much cared.

> —Louisa Alderman, *Everyday Chimera: Early Public Reaction to the Shade Epidemic*

Prologue

Out of the corner of his eye, Special Agent Gabriel Ruiz watched his new partner with serious trepidation. Stake-outs were never much fun, but being trapped in a hot sedan with a grown man who kept releasing little-girl sneezes was enough to make Ruiz give serious consideration to fed-on-fed violence.

He and Creadin were parked on a poorly lit dirt road on the outskirts of Heavenly, IL, a useless little town with a cannery, a bar, and a pathetic pharmacy that did triple-duty as the local post office and convenience store. They were situated on Main Street, facing the pharmacy, and as far as Ruiz could tell its main trade was selling cigarettes to teenagers working the cannery during the summer. He had already made a mental note not to buy any canned goods from that label. The store had closed at eight, and anyone left inside had simply wandered next door to the town's only bar, a dive called Benders.

Creadin unleashed another bout of darling "ah-choos"—there were always three in a row; it was god-damned precious—and shrugged helplessly, scrubbing his face with one palm like he was polishing his cheek-bones. "Allergies," he mumbled. "You gotta napkin or something in here?"

Ruiz shook his head in disgust. It better be allergies, he thought. He was not going to get sick because he got stuck in a car with one of the idiot newbies. "Use your sleeve, kid," he grumbled, keeping his eyes on the street. Granted, Creadin was in his midthirties, not even a decade younger than Ruiz, but he'd joined the Chicago branch just three weeks earlier. Another fuckup trans-ferring in from Counterterrorism. Between the recent killings and the agents who quit out of fear, half the office was new. Ruiz, on the other hand, had been with the di-vision since the day it opened.

He glared straight ahead, at their targets: a pack of teenagers standing on the sidewalk in front of the bar. The place definitely served beer to underage kids, and now several of them were standing in a loose circle out-side the bar, enjoying the cooling night air. The temper-ature that day had reached ninety-seven, with seventy percent humidity, and the air was only now starting to feel breathable. The kids were chatting and laughing, flirt-ing, stumbling a little, milking any excuse to lean on each other. They'd been doing it for over an hour now, and showed no signs of packing it in. None of them seemed the least bit concerned about the fact that adolescents in the area had recently disappeared into thin air.

Next to him, Creadin reached into the backseat and picked up the case file again, flipping it open and squinting at it in the dim light from the street. They had both been through the damn thing a dozen times already, but Creadin was compulsive about it by now, paging through the file the way some people might jiggle a knee or crack their knuckles. Six teens—that they knew of—had gone missing from three towns in this county, including Heavenly, in the last four months. Their division of the FBI, the newly created Bureau of Preternatural Investigations, had been called in after the third kid was attacked, when the local cops had actually managed to come up with a body: a seventeen-year-old girl named Bobbi Klay, who had bled out at the wrists. That itself wasn't enough to prove she'd been killed by a shade, but there were other signs: The body had multiple slices over major arteries, for example, and was wiped and moved after death. She'd obviously fought tooth and nail, judging by the defensive wounds on her hands and arms, but weakly, as if she'd lost a lot of blood before it occurred to her to protest. The pathologist who'd conducted the autopsy, Jessica Reyes, had suggested a shade attack.

That was when the BPI first stepped in, and right about when everything started going to hell. Three more kids had gone missing in the weeks after the BPI joined the investigation, and then four different *agents* suddenly disappeared. It was an enormous blow to the tiny and un-proven BPI. Unlike the rest of the Bureau, the supernatural division was organized into small teams of six agents, including a Senior Agent in Charge. There were only two pods on the East Coast and one in Chicago, but there was talk of opening another branch in Los Angeles, if Director Greene could get the funding. Losing four agents from the Chicago pod meant losing a large percentage of the entire BPI division, which made everyone look even worse.

Public perception was a whole other problem: In the months since the BPI's formation, all three pods had exhibited a nearly pathological lack of progress—hard proof that Greene could wave in front of Congress. Oh, they had discovered a number of alleged shades, both in Washington and here in the Chicago area, but every time the BPI found a trail it abruptly terminated. These people—these *things,* in Ruiz's opinion—could just fucking *vanish,* something that was otherwise impossible in the technological age. It was like playing goddamn Whac-a-Mole with murderers. No one had captured a shade, dead or alive, since Ambrose.

But now, thirty miles south of Chicago, the pattern had finally changed. The shades in question *had* to know the BPI was onto them, but they'd made no effort to back off. In fact, they'd only pushed harder, taken *more* kids, which went against every method they'd previously established. The Chicago SAC, Peralty, was so pissed he'd actually come out himself tonight, to run point out of the unmarked van two blocks over. It was a ballsy move, but also rather stupid, in Ruiz's opinion: The boss rarely made appearances in the field, and as a result everyone was discombobulated tonight.

As if Peralty could sense his disloyal thoughts, Ruiz's little Bluetooth earpiece beeped.

"Ruiz. Update." Peralty's voice was brusque, but Ruiz knew that was just to hide his anxiety. They *had* to find someone tonight, goddamn it. Too many people had died.

Ruiz lifted the radio. "More of the same, sir. . . . Wait—" As he watched, the kids began to break apart into groups. *Finally.* "They're splitting up now. Two couples are heading our way, and there's a group of three going west."

"Stay with the couples," Peralty instructed. "I'll send Hill and Ozmanski after the group."

"Yes, sir. Ruiz out." Ruiz started the sedan, while beside him Creadin let out one more round of cutesy sneezes before he flipped the file closed and fastened his seatbelt. They didn't speak, both too focused on the teenagers. Heavenly had plenty of streetlights, but unlike major cities, which gave off light from security doors and late-night businesses everywhere, in this Podunk town the street lamps were the only line of defense against the dark. As the kids walked from one pool of light into the next, there was always a quick moment where they were nearly invisible. It set Ruiz's teeth on edge.

He waited until the four kids had stumbled almost to the end of the block before he put the car in drive, creeping along the streets. When he was fifty feet behind them he pulled over again, waiting. In Chicago his behavior would have looked suspicious as hell, but the speed limit in downtown Heavenly was only twenty miles per hour. Everyone skulked around. And the kids were too caught up in their flirty conversations to pay any attention.

Ruiz followed the same procedure—letting them get ahead, skulking forward, pulling over—for two more blocks, and then the couples broke apart. Two of them stumbled up the sidewalk toward a dirt-brown Victorian residence with one light still on. They had their hands in each other's back pockets, laughing and intimate at the same time. They were obviously about two minutes away from getting naked. Ruiz grunted in disgust. Where were their goddamn *parents*? Didn't anyone in this town care that kids were disappearing?

Still, neither of them were shades, judging by the familiar body language and the certainty in their movements. These two had been dating awhile, and shades didn't do that, didn't get to know their victims first. Ruiz took his foot off the brake and continued after the remaining couple, with Creadin tense beside him.

The second couple—a short, muscled boy and a gangly girl three inches taller than him—chatted amiably as they walked, but they weren't touching. "Just friends, you think?" Creadin suggested.

"Or new acquaintances," Ruiz said grimly.

The guy suddenly turned and glanced over his shoulder, frowning at the unmarked BPI car. Then he gestured for the girl to turn a corner, walking the wrong way down a one-way street. "Fuck," Ruiz muttered, feeling the buzz of sudden adrenaline. "Where does that road go?" He had a rough understanding of the town's layout, but Creadin was the one who'd studied the maps.

"Couple of houses, an intersection, then it dumps into the cornfield." Like every other street in this godforsaken town. "Follow on foot?" the younger man asked.

"Yeah. Leave the jackets." Both men shucked their BPI Windbreakers, a relief in the hot air. Underneath, they were dressed in slacks and polo shirts, casual enough to blend in, at least at first glance. Ruiz reached into the backseat for a prop: a brown glass bottle in a paper bag. Empty, of course. "Let's go."

The two of them jogged through the steamy night to the corner where the kids had disappeared, and then slowed to an amble, beginning a conversation about the Cubs' new pitcher. Up ahead, Ruiz could just make out the figures of the two kids, still walking along, popping in and out of the light from the street lamps on Euclid. He felt the familiar tension of battle focus, and was so engaged with looking relaxed and maintaining the fake conversation that he almost jumped when the Bluetooth beeped again. Peralty's voice was suddenly shouting in his ear, "All units to the cornfield off . . . Euclid and Water Street!"

A block ahead of them. He and Creadin exchanged a quick glance and began to run forward. He looked ahead, at the kids, but they had vanished.

The bottle in its brown bag slipped from his fingers, but he was moving too fast to even hear it break. Creadin was faster than him, and Ruiz put on a burst of speed, trying to keep up. Despite his efforts Creadin was soon twenty feet ahead of him, across the street to the field of nine-foot-tall cornstalks. "There!" Creadin shouted, pointing to a hole where several stalks had been broken off. "They went this way!"

Ruiz took one quick look around him, checking for

an ambush, and when he looked back Creadin had disappeared into the corn.

"Fuck!" Ruiz screamed. Creadin wasn't a rookie; he should have known better than to go in there ahead of him. Ruiz pulled his flashlight out of his pocket and plunged in after his partner with his weapon in his right hand. He didn't even remember pulling the gun. He stopped just inside the cornfield, flashing the light in every direction, but there was no sign of Creadin. Just still stalks of corn that seemed to suck away the light.

He hit the Bluetooth. "Creadin! Get back here!" Silence. "Peralty?"

Ruiz heard shouting, not on the radio but way ahead of him in the corn, and he began to run, crashing through the dark cornfield with the gun muzzle pointed toward the ground and the flashlight held backward in his hand, so he could hold up one arm to shield his face. He did his best not to get hit by the heavy green ears that hung low on each cornstalk, but plenty of them banged into his shoulders and legs. The flashlight beam bounced in front of him, illuminating an aisle of dirt so narrow that Ruiz had to run at an angle, his wide-not-fat body tilted like a linebacker moving through an airplane.

"Where is everyone?" he shouted on the radio, just beginning to panic. The flashlight was serious—the latest model of 1,000 lumen CREE torch—but in the narrow space between rows it could only force out a small tunnel of bouncing light that had suddenly become Ruiz's whole world. Someone said something on the radio, and Ruiz skidded to a halt, trying to hear. "What? Hello?" There was a gurgling sound, and with both hands full he pressed his shoulder against his ear, trying to make it out. All he heard was a little bit of strangled breathing, and then the line went silent again. "Hey!" Ruiz shouted, breathing hard. He wasn't in *terrible* shape, but he wasn't exactly a regular at the gym, either. "Creadin! Peralty!" Nothing. "Hill! Where are you?"

Way down near where his flashlight beam ended, Ruiz saw something—someone—dart across his line of vision, running perpendicular through the corn. "Hey!" he shouted, raising the gun, but there was no answer. Ruiz was suddenly, overwhelmingly aware of his own vulnerability here. He was standing in the middle of a goddamned cornfield holding a flashlight as bright as a lighthouse, and there was likely at least one shade out here with him.

Instinctively, Ruiz clicked the light off and went still. He listened hard, working to control his breathing. Up until now he'd heard the occasional muffled cry or rustle of corn, but suddenly it was silent all around him. The air smelled of soil and green things that had baked all day in late-summer heat. He couldn't remember if he'd felt a breeze earlier today, but there sure as hell wasn't one now. The darkness and heat were too heavy; it was choking the air out of everything.

When he absolutely couldn't stand it any longer, he clicked on his flashlight. And screamed.

The shade was standing three feet in front of him, close enough to touch, peering at him through long, stringy blond hair that had a foot of pink at the bottom. Bright red blood dripped down her chin, and there was more blood streaked down her tank top and cutoff shorts. It matched the red of her irises and pupils. She only looked about eighteen, but she was holding something like a miniature machete, twirling it around in her right hand with the comfort of decades of practice. She smiled at him, a wide scarlet grin that sent urine running down Ruiz's pants leg.

"Hello," she chirped, like a cheerful clerk at a candy store. She raised a bloody hand and wiggled her fingers at him. "I'm Giselle. What's your name?"

"I'm—" he began, and then raised his weapon and squeezed the trigger twice, hoping it would throw her off balance. But the shade just evaporated into the corn.

Her voice came from somewhere to his left. "You got a shot off. Very good!" His pistol swung wildly as he pointed it left and right, trying to find the source of the sound, but she was moving. Something rustled behind him, and he whipped around, gun up—only to see an empty row of corn. He faced the original direction again, terrified that she was about to pop out at him, but instead of shade claws he saw . . . a pile of something. It had been dropped about thirty feet down the row of corn. Had that been there before? He hadn't looked past the woman. Ruiz stepped closer, pointing the light right at it, and realized he was looking at bodies. He spotted Hill's short brunette haircut, and Creadin's sightless eyes, and the horror swept over him.

"If you survive this," came the conversational voice, from somewhere to his left, "please tell your people to leave us alone. They can't stop what's coming." She was close now, only a few feet away, and Ruiz took one slow step backward as she began to crouch. Then some instinct alerted him, and he swung the flashlight beam just up in time to see her descending on him like an angel from hell.

Chapter 1

"Tell me again why you would ever want to take this job, Special Agent McKenna."

Alex squirmed in his seat, unaccustomed to having to sit still for so long. He'd been interviewing for the promotion all day, working his way up the chain to Deputy Director Marcia Harding.

"I feel that I'm the best person to implement the FBI's evolving mission in Chicago," he began again. "The operational changes require a dedicated field agent, not just a supervisor—"

Harding's eyes narrowed. "Cut the shit, Alex. I didn't ask you what the job requires, I asked you why you want it. Why on earth would you want to transfer into the BPI at this point in your career?"

Alex opened his mouth to start again, but before he could speak she added, "And don't tell me what you think I want to hear. I changed your diapers, I can tell if you're lying to me."

"Yes, ma'am." Alex took a breath, composing his thoughts. Unlike the last two interviewers, Harding had known him for years. She wasn't about to just hand over the gig, even knowing no one else wanted it. "I don't agree with what the media is suggesting about the BPI," he said carefully. "The director wouldn't have created the division if she didn't think the threat from shades was a serious one. I know that internally we consider the BPI a place to send fu—er, screwups and trainees, but I think this division is going to be as important to the Bureau as Counterterrorism was in the early 2000s, or Cyber in the 2010s."

She nodded, the suspicious expression finally beginning to clear up a little. Harding was in her midfifties, a naturally rounded woman with short gray hair and gray eyes that had cut right through Alex since she'd babysat him as a child. The trainees had bestowed the rather obvious nickname of "Bureau Battle-ax."

"Go on," she said.

Alex leaned forward in the visitor's chair, ticking off points on his fingers. "First off, if I get this job, I'll be the youngest SAC in the BPI. Even my mother wasn't a SAC until her late thirties. Secondly, the shades interest me. You know that I majored in biology; I think the science aspect is fascinating. Finally, if I can straighten out this mess in Chicago, I'll have made my bones in the agency. I'm tired of everyone assuming nepotism got me here." *And just a little afraid it's true,* he thought, but knew better than to say out loud.

Harding cocked a pewter eyebrow. "Ambition? That's your reason? People are dying. *Agents* are dying, and we're no closer to understanding why the shades have changed their behavior. Surely a promotion can't be worth running straight into a death sentence."

"Of course not," Alex said. "But I don't plan to get killed."

"Neither did any of the others." She sighed heavily. "Your mother wouldn't want this, Alex. She wouldn't have wanted you to put your life in even greater danger just to climb the Bureau ladder."

Alex felt himself tensing. "With respect, Deputy Director, my mother is dead. She doesn't want or not want anything anymore. But the fact that she was never a part of the BPI, never a part of the shade investigations, that's exactly why I want to go."

Harding tapped her blunt fingernails against her desk for a moment, eyeing him. Alex fought not to start fidgeting. He could tell from Harding's face that she wasn't convinced. "Did you see the *Post* this morning?" she asked finally.

He nodded. "They're calling for the Chicago BPI pod

to be disbanded altogether. But that can't be something you're seriously considering."

She just stared at him for a moment, and Alex had to bite down on his indignation. "Ma'am, agents aside, those shades have taken six teenagers and outright killed another. How could the Bureau just let that go?"

"There's no conclusive evidence tying the disappearances to the shades," she pointed out. Before Alex could respond, she raised a hand and added, "I know, the murder of that teenage girl was almost certainly a shade attack, but the outright disappearances ... it's all conjecture. And regardless, it makes the Bureau look bad. Between you and me, there's a debate within this building right now, over letting the shades have Chicago."

Alex wanted to jump up and start yelling, but he managed to contain it. "Ma'am, no. I know the media is all over this case—"

"Which actually works against you," she cut in. "Look at it from the public's perspective. How does it look if we send our legacy agent to Chicago to be slaughtered?"

Alex flinched at the phrasing. *TIME* magazine had done a big article on him two years earlier, the last time he'd been promoted. The piece was titled "Special Agent Legacy," and Alex still hadn't lived it down. To this day a copy surfaced in his life every few days, taped to his front door or left under his windshield wiper.

"I *am* looking at it from the public's perspective, ma'am," he countered. "If you send me to Chicago, it shows the media that you're taking this threat seriously, that you're not afraid of the shades. *That* is the message you want to send, not 'We couldn't handle it so we just left.'"

She glared at him for another instant, and then her face softened. "If something happens to you, it'll be my responsibility."

"Look at it this way," he offered, trying a grin, "if you don't send me, and something else happens to Chicago, it'll be your responsibility, too."

The deputy director couldn't help smiling back. "You're incorrigible. Always were."

"Yes, ma'am. But I'm still the best agent for this job. And," he couldn't resist adding, "I'm guessing you haven't had a whole lot of other applicants."

She sighed and closed the file. "I assume you want to take Eddy with you?"

"Yes, ma'am. He's in the building now; he came along to see friends in D.C."

She gave him a wry smile. "Fine. At least he'll have your back. I'll inform your supervisor in Philadelphia and start the paperwork. Go through the files right away. I want you in Chicago by Sunday."

Sunday? That was fast—fast enough that Alex suspected she'd made up her mind before he'd walked in there. Harding rose, beginning to extend her right arm, but then with a little "what the hell" wave she came around the desk and embraced him. Surprised at the breach in decorum, Alex hugged her back. "Don't get dead," Harding told him.

~

Alex strode down the familiar hallway, managing not to fist pump. He nodded hellos at a few of the older guys, the ones who had served here during his mother's tenure as director. Alex had practically grown up at the Hoover building, or it felt like it anyway. When he was a kid his aunt had often brought him to this building when his mom had to work late, so they could drop off dinner and Alex could get a kiss before bedtime. Every trip to FBI headquarters had become the focal point for that day, and all the days before and after, until the next visit. It was good to be back, however briefly.

Alex's best friend was waiting for him at the reception desk, talking on his cell phone. Chase Eddy just rolled his eyes, holding up a finger. Alex crossed his arms over his best black suit, waiting.

"I know, baby, but I'm in D.C. with Alex for the weekend," Chase was saying. "I'll call you next week, though."

"No you won't," Alex interjected.

Chase glared at him and said into the phone, "I know, I can't wait to see you, either."

"Yes you can," Alex said.

After a quick glance to make sure they were alone, Chase leaned back and mimed a karate kick. Alex just smirked at him.

Chase eyed the expression for a moment, and then his face fell. He hung up the phone and put it in a pocket. "You got it," he said, sounding resigned.

Alex grinned. "I got it. *We* got it. Harding said you can be my number two." He raised a smug eyebrow, daring Chase to take the bait, but his friend just shook his head, still looking dejected. Alex grabbed his shoulder, steering him toward the exit. "Come on, you can buy me lunch to celebrate."

"Ugh. Fine. McDonald's it is," Chase said, still looking morose.

There wasn't actually a McDonald's nearby, but they walked two blocks to Heroes, a sandwich bistro with decent, if overpriced, food. It was always populated with plenty of FBI agents and staff, and Alex found himself waving several times before they could place orders. When they had been seated in a window booth, Chase asked in an airy tone, "So what makes you think I even want to follow you to Chicago?"

"Um, let's see. It's a promotion, and you'll make more money. You love money, and you hate Philly. Plus, you'll get to work for your best friend," Alex said, ticking off the points on his fingers.

"Oh, you're not my best friend," Chase corrected. "I'm obviously *your* best friend, but I have many other social options I choose not to talk about."

Alex ignored this, his foot jiggling up and down with excitement. "Come on, man. Ride my coattails. It'll be fun."

Chase didn't smile. "Seriously, Alex. We could die out there."

"We could die anywhere," Alex pointed out. "Don't you want it to be somewhere with deep-dish pizza?"

Chase looked at him for a long moment, then finally shook his head, acquiescing. "All right. You had me at 'deep-dish pizza.'"

"Whatever, man. You're as curious about these things as I am."

"Maybe," Chase replied. "Or maybe I just figure you've got a better chance of staying alive with me there."

"Touché."

"How fast is this gonna happen?" Chase asked. "I mean, Harding puts in the paperwork, then what, a couple weeks to get packed up and move? We gonna get a U-Haul and drive out there, or—" He broke off. "Alex, I do not like the look on your face right now."

Alex swallowed his massive bite of French fries, looking guilty. "About that," he began.

~

Four hours later, Alex and Chase had nearly covered the large conference table in one of the Bureau's many meeting rooms. The FBI was as dazzled by the idea of a paper-free society as any other large organization, but they still believed in building paper files for employees and applicants. Little by little the piles of rejected agents had grown and migrated down the table, while the stacks of prospects dwindled bleakly.

Pickings were slim. Only a couple of weeks earlier, the BPI had been flooded with requests for transfers. Shade investigation had briefly been considered the hot new track in the Bureau, and Chicago was a desirable office. After so many agents had been killed, however, many applicants had called to withdraw, and the stacks of files had dwindled to about twenty. Most of them fell into one of two groups: the hardcore anti-shade activists—people who referred to them as the "vampire plague"—or the Bureau's serious troublemakers, agents who were desperate to transfer out of a bad situation, usually of their own design.

Alex didn't have any problem with hating shades, but hardcore obsessives rarely made good team members, in his experience. He was slightly more forgiving of "troublemakers" than the average agent, being keenly aware of how unfairly reputations could be made, but there was a science to picking a cohesive team, and putting in too many cowboys wasn't going to help them stay alive.

And that was part of the problem, he'd realized: figuring out how to stay alive. Alex had put teams together before, on temporary operations and a couple of minor task forces he'd run, but this was the first time he was faced with having real, immediate power over not just careers, but lives. Nine agents had been killed so far, enough that the rest of the BPI was calling the Chicago office "Death's Waiting Room." Alex was all too aware he could be choosing people to die. They needed three competent agents, although four would be better. Then they could get someone to sub in for a month or two until Ruiz was back on duty. But both Alex and Chase were scrambling to come up with even one.

"Okay, I want this guy, Bartell," Alex said finally, moving one of the files to a rare clean patch of table. "He was in on the first shade case, Ambrose. Helped design the cell they still keep him in."

"He's fifty-five," Chase pointed out, looking over Alex's shoulder. "Two years to retirement?"

"He's *experienced.*"

Chase shrugged. "Okay, fine. At least he doesn't have a family. What about this one?" He slapped open a file. "Jill Hadley. She's a star with the Chicago FBI, applied for a transfer last year and hasn't pulled it since the killings. On the contrary, she's e-mailed Harding's assistant twice to remind him that she's still interested."

Alex examined the file, noting the attached picture of a slender woman with red hair so long it might have touched her navel. "You get that you can't sleep with her, right?"

"Grow up, man. She's hungry, and she'll know the town."

Alex held up his hands. "Okay, okay. That's two," He picked up Hadley's file and set it on top of Bartell's. "We need one more."

Chase frowned at the piles around him. "All of these are losers."

"Well, which one of those losers will be the biggest asset?"

"None of them are all that great, far as I can tell," Chase grumbled. "Unless, of course, you're purely looking for cannon fodder. . . ." He made a show of eyeing the piles with sudden interest.

"No, I think they've killed enough of us." Alex sat back in his chair and surveyed the files. "But you're right.

We need to think outside the box. And that means more intelligence on shades themselves."

"Good luck with that. Every agency in the world's been working on it."

Alex thought about it for a few minutes, absently tapping out a rhythm on the table. What the Chicago pod *really* needed was a fresh angle. "Maybe they have," Alex said slowly, "but we have something most of them don't."

"What's that?"

"We can go see Ambrose."

Chase snorted. "To what end? He won't tell us anything. Do you know how many agents have tried? And last I checked Congress still hasn't gotten around to declaring him inhuman." According to the law, the shade was technically still a US citizen, which meant he couldn't be tortured or even studied invasively. Ambrose had a team of exorbitantly priced lawyers who made sure of it. The Bureau labs had gotten permission to draw blood and collect hair and saliva samples, but anything else was off the table until Congress got around to declaring him inhuman. Even then, Ambrose was so high profile, it was unlikely they'd get away with physically torturing him for information as long as he was on US soil. He was too famous now.

Still, plenty of agents had taken a run at interrogating Ambrose through his two-inch-thick plexiglass cell—not to mention Bureau psychologists, biologists, and MDs. Ambrose had proven himself impervious to all of the Bureau's forms of psychological manipulation, and they were pretty good at that kind of thing. If Alex wanted to get anything out of him, he would need to get creative. Trouble was, every FBI agent in the world spent years being trained how to think the way the Bureau wanted. Even out-of-the-box thinking was according to Bureau specifications.

Unable to remain still any longer, Alex got up and paced the conference room. Chase, who had worked with him for over a decade, just pushed back in his chair, stretched, and waited him out. "Make the call to Camp Vamp," Alex said finally. "I'll think of something."

Chapter 2

One good thing about being the new Chicago SAC, Alex thought a few hours later, was you could get things done in a hurry.

By eight o'clock that night he and Chase had arrived at the National Security Branch building, where they met Lucius Tymer, the high-level SAC in charge of the care and keeping of the Bureau's most famous prisoner. When Alex was a teenager Tymer had been a notorious Bureau cowboy, someone his mother had to call on the carpet at least once a month. As he got older—Tymer was a couple months shy of fifty—he'd drifted away from insubordination and taken an interest in oddities: female serial killers, complex international kidnappings, and yes, reports of otherworldly creatures who had abilities beyond normal humans. By the time Ambrose was captured, Tymer had already spent a couple of years looking into these sightings. He'd volunteered to run the first,

D.C.-based BPI pod, the one devoted specifically to Ambrose's confinement and study. Alex suspected Tymer would be studying shades right up until retirement—unless, God forbid, something even weirder came along.

Tymer was a collector: His primary interest was the acquisition of anomalies. With that in mind, he'd made a point to keep tabs on the career of Alex McKenna, the legacy agent. When Alex got on the phone with him, Tymer had already heard about the promotion, despite it being less than five hours old, and he readily agreed to let the newly minted SAC visit Ambrose later that evening—though he balked at letting Chase Eddy join Alex during the interrogation. "We rarely allow more than one person in front of him at a time," Tymer explained. "We don't feed him as often as he'd like, so when there's extra blood around he gets overstimulated, like a toddler in a candy store. Makes it hard for him to focus on the questions." There was a pause, and then the senior agent added, "We always keep two spotters at the end of the hall, though, staring right at you for any signs of compulsion. I'll act as one, and Eddy can join me."

Tymer was waiting for them at the first checkpoint, a broad-shouldered black man of average height, a little more rotund than Alex remembered, although it had been a couple of years. He had a scar on his throat and several more on his hands and forearms, defensive wounds from various street-level battles during his early years with the FBI. Tymer was a bit vain about the scars—the man had a reputation for going around in rolled-up shirtsleeves even in the dead of winter. "Alex," he said warmly. "Good to see you again, my boy. Congratulations on the promotion."

"Thank you, sir." Alex shook his hand and gestured to Chase. "You've met Agent Eddy, I believe? He's going to be my number two in Chicago."

"Right, of course." Tymer, who appeared to be just noticing the other agent's existence, shook Chase's hand as well. "I'm glad you boys could stop by before you take off. Gives me a chance to show off the little we've learned."

"We're anxious to see if he can shed any light on the situation in Chicago, sir," Alex said, just to remind Tymer that this wasn't a tourist visit.

"Right, right." Tymer eyed him. "You got papers or something to show him?"

Alex nodded and held up a file folder. "Stuff from Chicago. We're hoping he'll detect a pattern."

Tymer held out his hand, and Alex gave him the folder. He flipped through it, removing several staples and a paper clip from the group of photos. He sighed heavily as he handed it back. "Well, those should get his motor running. We'll deal with it, though. I know the kind of pressure you're facing." Alex nodded and thanked him. The other BPI agents might have seen him as a dead man walking, but none of them wanted to be the guy who made things harder for the new agent in charge of the Chicago debacle.

Tymer led Alex and Chase through the first, general security check, the same one used by all building visitors. Then all three men moved toward a nondescript stairway that led to the basement—or what was known in-house as Camp Vamp. At the bottom of the stairway was a second checkpoint, which appeared to be a few tables set up to form a sort of *U* shape that closed off the hallway except for a slim opening, just wide enough for Tymer to squeeze through. Two female lab techs in white coats and surgical masks sat behind the table, fussing with equipment that Alex didn't recognize. "Now, this here," Tymer said with pride, "is my own brainchild. After the first escape attempt, our biggest concern was that a shade would either break in here or transmute one of our own agents, send him in to get Ambrose out. But as you probably know, we've yet to develop a decent blood test for codifying humans and shades."

Alex nodded. "Shade and human blood samples are similar all the way down to the DNA code, and that can take days to run." Since Ambrose's capture the previous year, every DNA lab in the country was backlogged.

Tymer smiled, pleased. "Exactly. Our labs just aren't fast enough, and my advisors say it'll be a couple of years yet before we can put together an instant blood test. We spent the first six months trying to develop a high-tech test," he explained as he held his badge and ID up to the first technician. "Something that could work at the speed we needed. Finally I realized we were overthinking it." He paused, turning back to face Alex and Chase. "Are you aware of how we feed Ambrose?" he asked abruptly.

Alex knew, but he tilted his body a little, indicating that Chase should step forward and join the conversation. "Blind donation from a bloodmobile," Chase said, and Tymer gave him a pleased nod as if he were a star pupil at Quantico. Really, anyone with a newspaper would know how Ambrose was fed, because it had sparked quite the public debate a few months earlier. When biologists had finally confirmed that yes, Subject A did require human blood in order to survive, thousands of weirdos had rushed forward with offers to donate, hoping to be personally fed on by a vampire. At the same time, thousands of protestors had come forward claiming that there was no way in hell their tax dollars should do anything to help the evil filth survive. The BPI and a special police task force racked up overtime trying to get the two sides to calm down, while working on the thorny ethical issue of drawing blood from a free citizen and giving it to a federal prisoner.

The quandary was eventually solved by the Red Cross, of all things. The company's spokeswoman came forward and suggested that a permanent blood drive location could be set up specifically for the vampire groupies. From that supply, Ambrose would receive his minimal nutritional requirements, and the rest would be donated to the many good causes for which the Red Cross provided blood. The BPI decided to give it a three-month trial run, and the Red Cross reported exponential gains in blood donation, enough to nearly meet blood requirements at East Coast hospitals, for the first time in the history of the organization. These results eventually reduced the anti-vampire brigade to grumbles and mutters, which was a hell of a lot better than the street riots that had previously been threatened.

"In every donation scenario," Tymer went on, "there is a certain percentage of blood that simply can't be used, because of the donor's illness, health risks, and so on." He smiled smugly. "We take possession of that excess, and use it for the simplest test imaginable." He waved toward the lab tech, who pressed on one of the large containers, which was roughly the size and shape of a small copy machine. A door panel popped out, and she reached in and pulled out what looked like an especially high-quality Tupperware container, completely transparent. Inside, Alex could see a thick red liquid sloshing around, and his stomach churned just a little. Blood. He wasn't one of those people who fainted at the sight of it, but he wasn't an enormous fan, either.

The second tech handed the first woman what looked like a gas mask with a long tube running out of the bottom. The first tech connected it to a valve in the top of the container. She handed it to Tymer, who donned the mask with practiced motions. When it was secured on the back of his head, he took a deep breath, in and out, which the first tech followed on a handheld monitoring device. After the breath, the second tech leaned over the table with a flashlight, shining it at Tymer's eyes while he stood there complacently. Both techs nodded, and Tymer peeled the gas mask off.

"That's it?" Alex said, incredulous. "You just inhale . . . what, blood fumes?"

Tymer grinned. "That's it. We got the lawyer's permission to try this on Ambrose—which was a huge pain in the ass from a security standpoint, by the way—and every single time, he exhibits the stimulation response." He motioned to his own eyes to indicate what the press loved to call "vamping out," when blood drained into a shade's irises and pupils to indicate their awakened blood hunger. Ambrose had done it a couple of times on national television. "We've tested different amounts of blood, using control substances instead of human blood, trying him at different times of day, everything our scientists could think of. We've tinkered enough to get this thing damn near perfect—*if* you've got about three liters of human blood lying around. It will withstand a certain amount of refrigeration, although we've found that after about a month it loses some of its . . . allure. That's why we keep getting the fresh stuff."

"What if he holds his breath?" Chase asked. "Fakes breathing?"

In answer, the first tech held up her monitoring device. "I'll see that here. We can monitor the air pressure in the tube."

"Smart," Chase said approvingly.

"Jesus," Alex blurted. "If the private sector finds out about that . . ."

Tymer's face turned grave. "I know. The world's most secure corporations are already requiring DNA tests from new employees. If this gets out they could create a whole new market for selling blood, which is desperately needed by hospitals already. That's why we're keeping it quiet." He motioned for Alex and Chase to step forward, and each took a turn breathing into the mask. When they had passed the test, the two women waved them through the narrow space between the wall and the table.

Chase eyed the simple setup. "No offense, but the checkpoint doesn't look all that imposing," he commented.

"It's not supposed to. We *want* one of these assholes to take a run at springing Ambrose, so we can have another specimen. Aw, hell. Let me show you." He nodded at the female tech, who must have pressed some sort of silent alarm, though Alex barely saw her arm twitch. A siren blared, and Alex looked up to see lights flashing in the ceiling. By the time his eyes moved down again, he was looking down the barrel of a Micro Desert Eagle wielded by the woman who'd gotten the blood out of the cooler. Adrenaline spiking, Alex raised his hands, and Chase did the same beside him. He was dimly aware of the sound of running behind him, and realized there were several armed agents there as well. They were trapped.

"These aren't technicians," Tymer said proudly, motioning to the woman in front of Alex. "Rebecca here is my finest marksman." He shot her an apologetic glance. "Er, markswoman. Sorry, Bex."

The woman gave a good-natured eye roll and holstered the sidearm, reaching up with her free hand to pull down the surgical mask, exposing a grin. She peeled off her surgical glove and held out her hand. "Agent Rebecca Lanver, sir. Good to meet you."

Alex shook, introducing himself and then Chase. Seeing the opportunity to talk to someone other than Tymer, he asked Lanver how often they ran the agents through the test.

"Every day. The process is so simple that every agent in the pod can administer it," she answered. "We test each other every single morning, and when we have someone coming in to see the subject, we take turns on checkpoint duty."

"Not bad, right?" Tymer grinned proudly, and Alex and Chase exchanged a glance. Alex was pretty sure Chase was thinking what he was—could they replicate the test in Chicago? It was definitely something to think about.

It took a few minutes to de-escalate the false alarm, and then Tymer walked them through the third and final checkpoint, where Alex and Chase surrendered their guns and badges. "We had an agent last year who was one of those Champions of Humanity assholes," Tymer said, rolling his eyes at the mention of the anti-shade religious lobbyists. "Got right past all our background checks somehow. He actually snuck in there with his gun and got a couple of shots at Ambrose. The idiot failed to realize that three-inch plexiglass can keep bullets out as well as it keeps the shade in. Got himself right in the kneecap with the ricochet."

"I didn't hear about that," Alex said, surprised.

"You wouldn't have. The powers that be hushed it up but good. BPI's got enough media problems without them finding out one of our own was a wing nut." He motioned for them to keep emptying their pockets, until Alex had given up his phone, wallet, and even spare change. He raised his eyebrows at Tymer.

"He'll try to mesmerize you right away," the older agent explained. "He *should* need the saliva, but we've discovered that about one in every hundred people is just naturally susceptible to it, enough that he can get you on visual cues alone. There's no way to break him out from this side, but if he gets you to pass any of your stuff through the airlock he'll make a pest of himself so we have to come in and take it away."

He let them keep their belts and shoelaces—"Your spotter would see you taking that stuff off in time to stop you"—and the three of them went through the final door into Camp Vamp.

The door opened onto a short entryway with bright fluorescent lighting. Just inside the door was a desk with ten monitors—nine of them dark—and a spotter's chair, positioned so the occupant could see both the monitor and the short corridor of plexiglass cells beyond. The basement had been renovated for this purpose shortly after Ambrose's second escape attempt, when he'd managed to spit shade saliva through cell bars in a guard's eyes.

There were five cells on each side of the hallway, with Ambrose as the only occupant. "He's in the fourth cell on the left," Tymer said quietly. "The rooms are sound-proofed, but we don't quite trust it, given how little we know about their enhanced senses. Anything you don't want him to know, don't say. We've got a one-way mirror in front of the plexiglass, but we can turn it on and off so the prisoner can see out." He nodded to a control panel on the wall near the door. "When Alex gets down there I'll hit the control, so Ambrose can see him. We've got audio here"—he handed Chase a set of headphones, picking up a second pair for himself—"and we'll be recording as well, just in case. If the spotter sees anything off, or either of us thinks you're getting mesmerized, I'll hit the control and he'll have a one-way mirror again. Understood?"

"Yes, sir." Alex held up the folder. "And this?"

"Right. I'd advise you to just hold it up to the plexiglass if you can, but he'll want you to send it through the airlock. That's fine—let him have a win—but know that anything you give him, he's not giving back. We'll have to retrieve it on his next scheduled cell cleaning." He clapped Alex on the shoulder and handed him a plastic folding chair. "Good luck, son."

Alex didn't like that *son,* but he managed to resist

shrugging the other man's hand off as he took the lightweight chair. He was suddenly nervous. Chase gave him a nod of encouragement. "If the guy says anything about fava beans or Chianti, get out of there," he advised solemnly. Alex made a face and turned to walk down the hallway to face the vampire.

~

The cells on either side of Alex were sparse: a small bed, a metal toilet, and an airlock for sending materials back and forth. Before he'd passed the first pair he felt unnerved by the quiet. He had visited a number of prisons, and every single one of them had been cacophonous. This place was clean, new looking, brightly lit, and completely silent. It was creepy as hell.

He reached Ambrose's cell with images from *The Silence of the Lambs* still at the forefront of his mind, thanks to Chase. When he turned to face the shade he was surprised to find the occupied cell just as bare as the three he'd already passed. No artwork, no photos, no stacks of mail. No sharp edges anywhere. Everything had been taken away. As a punishment? Or had Ambrose not wanted anything in there with him?

Alex's eyes automatically scanned for any movement, which was how he missed Ambrose on the first pass. He had to look through the room a second time before he saw the man standing absolutely still in the back corner, leaning against the beige walls as if he were painted with camouflage. Which he might as well have been: Ambrose was dressed in an off-white jumpsuit, his small square features perfectly still and blank. The shade was average height; he had brown hair and a face that was sort of blandly pleasant rather than handsome or homely. Other than the stillness, Ambrose just looked like any normal guy you'd see at a bar or a business meeting. Alex had seen photos, of course, but he realized in that moment that he'd been expecting the shade to give off an otherworldly vibe in person: some sort of alien quality that immediately identified him as nonhuman. It was a stupid idea, really. The shades would never have made it this long without being able to blend in perfectly. There might have been a hint of predator about him, but no more than you'd see with Wall Street assholes aggressively hitting on women at a bar.

Tymer must have flicked the switch for the mirror, because suddenly the fluorescent lighting in Ambrose's cell shifted, and the shade gave a sudden blink, looking around as if he'd been caught in a daydream, until his raptor eyes landed on Alex. There was a sudden blur of motion, and then the shade was just *there,* standing directly in front of Alex on the other side of the plexiglass. Alex couldn't help but give a little start, nearly dropping the chair, and he saw the shade smirk with triumph.

"So sorry about that, Agent," he said. "I didn't meant to startle you."

"Sure you did." Alex said easily. "But that's fine. I'd probably be looking for entertainment, too, if I had to be in that cell all day."

The shade frowned, looking Alex up and down. "I thought they were done with sending new people to test me."

"I'm Alex," he said. "You mind if I sit down?" He held up the plastic folding chair, and Ambrose shrugged. "Thanks." Alex unfolded the seat and settled himself into it, giving Ambrose a moment to look him over. The shade remained standing on the other side of the plexiglass with an unreadable expression. Alex made sure his own face was relaxed, though it felt surreal to sit across from the vampire, like something out of a bad horror movie.

"If you don't mind, Mr. Ambrose, I'd like to ask you a few questions about your culture," he began. "Are the shades organized? Do they have a central leader? Can you communicate with each other?"

Ambrose just stared at him silently, his arms hanging a little loose from his body. "You've been asked all that before, huh?" Alex said with a smile. "That must get annoying."

The shade just cocked an eyebrow and looked point-edly at the file in Alex's hand. "Oh, this?" Alex said. "These are some photos. Shade murders, or so we think. I was hoping you might help me figure out who did it." Without waiting for a reply, he stood up and began laying out photos and documents on the floor, right up against the plexiglass. Ambrose glanced down at them with re-luctance, as though he wanted to resist but couldn't help himself. The color photos caught his eye, and he soon began moving along the wall on his side, studying the images.

"That one," he said abruptly, his finger jabbing at a color photo of the pile of dead BPI agents in the corn-field. "Send me that one."

There was a small airlock fixed into the plexiglass at waist height, along the right side of the cell. It was about the size and width of a ream of paper. Alex went over and opened the door on his side of the plexiglass, placing the photo inside. Ambrose's hand darted for his own door, but it wouldn't open until Alex closed his. He waited un-til the shade met his eyes. "Why that shot?" he asked qui-etly. "You just looking to add to the spank bank?"

Ambrose licked his lips. "Maybe. Or maybe I recog-nize the work."

Alex shut his side of the airlock door and let the shade have the picture. He ripped it out, examining it from three inches away. Alex saw a faint reddish cast come over Ambrose's eyes. He was . . . stimulated.

Time for an experiment. "Giselle," Alex said softly.

Ambrose looked up, startled. Realizing he'd already given himself away, the shade nodded. "She identified herself to you?"

"Not me," Alex replied. "The surviving agent."

Ambrose's eyebrows rose a fraction. "She left a survivor? Interesting. He must have impressed her."

To Alex's surprise, Ambrose jammed the photo back in the airlock and slammed his door closed, sending it back. "I can't help you," he said with finality.

"Just tell me a little more about Giselle."

"No."

"I can make your stay here easier," Alex offered. "Reading material, maybe a television. I might even be able to talk them into increasing your feeding schedule."

Ambrose eyes flickered at the last suggestion, but he shook his head hard. "I have been in this box for ten months," he said, anger in his voice. "Do you think you're the first one to come in here and offer that? Or even the sixth? Nothing you can offer would be worth that."

He put the slightest emphasis on the word *that,* and Alex went still. Why would information about Giselle be more valuable than any other? On a hunch, he asked, "Who does she work for?"

Ambrose immediately turned his back and stalked over to the bed, lying down facing the wall. He almost seemed . . . *scared.*

"Okay, fine," Alex said. "Don't tell me about Giselle, or her boss. Give me someone else. A name. Another shade I can push instead."

No response. Ambrose didn't even lift his head. Alex glanced to left, to where Tymer and Chase were watching. Chase gave a little shrug: *Now what?* Tymer looked as if this was exactly what he'd expected. He made a little motion for Alex to come back to the door.

But Alex turned back to the plexiglass, thinking. They needed this. They needed *something,* anyway. He couldn't touch Ambrose, certainly couldn't torture him. There was nothing to threaten him with, either, and any offered bribe would be just a promise, at this point. What was the promise of future reward against something that Ambrose seemed to be actively afraid of, even in here? Alex glanced at the plexiglass barrier, the airlock. He had an idea, God help him.

He turned back to the door and gave Chase a significant look, one that his friend had dubbed "Alex's 'Keep Me out of Jail, Buddy' face." Chase caught it and took an uncertain step forward. "Alex, don't—"

Before he could think about what he was about to do, Alex opened the buckle on his belt and pulled the little prong forward. "McKenna!" came Tymer's brusque voice, but Alex ignored him, not wanting to lose his nerve.

He jammed the pad of his thumb over the belt prong, hard enough for the metal to hit bone, gritting his teeth against the pain. With his other hand he opened the airlock door and stuck his hand inside, feeling the blood spurt out.

Tymer started shouting, but out of the corner of his eye Alex could see that Chase had stepped in front of the older agent, talking to him in low tones, one hand on his shoulder. Trusting his partner, Alex turned his gaze back to Ambrose, who had rolled over as soon as he heard the tinkle of the belt. Seeing what Alex was doing, Ambrose streaked across the cell and was suddenly in front of the airlock on his knees, his nose pressed against the crack. He gave a soft moan, his fingernails prying at the edges.

Alex blinked in surprise. He hadn't expected *that* big of a reaction, but hadn't Tymer said they fed Ambrose rarely? Was the shade starving? Or was it the difference between warm, live blood, and donated blood from a refrigerator? Either way, Alex needed to press his advantage.

"Who does Giselle work for?" he asked insistently, but Ambrose shook his head, wailing, "I can't, I can't . . ."

Alex let that go on for a second, hearing the voices near the entrance getting heated. Tymer was gonna stomp over there any second. "Then give me a name,"

Alex ordered. "Another shade who might know."

Ambrose lifted his head, and Alex saw that the shade's face was mottled with need, his eyes bright red. The skin around his eyes seemed to have shrunken inward, veins popping. "Please . . ." he moaned. There was a decent-sized puddle of blood in the airlock, so Alex pulled off his cheap tie and drew his hand out, wrapping the tie around the wound—but not before a couple extra drops of blood hit the floor. Ambrose's eyes were glued to them.

"A name," Alex insisted.

A calculating glint flashed through those red eyes, and despite the "stimulation response," Alex recognized it from dozens of other interviews with suspects: The shade had thought of someone he could throw under the bus. "Rosalind Frederick," he blurted.

"City?"

"Cincinnati!"

Alex closed the little airlock door, and Ambrose opened his so hard that it ripped off in his hand. The shade thrust his whole face up against it, licking frantically at the blood, sticking his fingers in to swipe up every last drop.

~

"So, thanks for that," Chase said sarcastically as they were escorted out by a grim-looking Agent Lanver. There must have been another set of monitors in a control room somewhere, or maybe she just didn't like it when her boss was unhappy, but she was practically frog-marching them out the door. "I thought Tymer was gonna break my neck. Do you know how many laws you just broke?"

"Not that many," Alex said mildly. "Congress hasn't gotten around to writing shade laws yet, remember?"

Chase snorted. "That doesn't mean his lawyers aren't going to go apeshit over that little stunt."

Alex shrugged, clutching his thumb with the tie wrapped around it. It was still bleeding a little, and he tried to remember when he'd had his last tetanus shot. "You were the one who told me to figure out a way to keep us alive in Chicago. Now we have new information—"

"You make it sound so simple," Lanver broke in angrily. "We've spent ten months developing a system and a schedule with the subject, and all the security precautions and all the drills, and you just come in and drop a hand grenade and waltz off."

"I rarely waltz," Alex intoned. She glowered at him in response, and he sighed, stopping and turning all the way around to face her. They were right by the first entrance checkpoint, and a few people sent curious looks their way: a furious woman and a man with a bloody tie. "Look," Alex said, as sincerely as he could, "I know I just caused you guys some problems, and I'm sorry about that. But look at it this way: I exploited a weakness that you now know about, and the only person who got hurt was me."

"That's not—argh!" She sighed loudly and stalked away. Alex thought she was heading back down to Tymer, but she went over to the security guard at the checkpoint, spoke to him for a second, and reached behind the counter.

"Watch out, man," Chase murmured, his voice amused. "She's probably getting a Taser to teach you a lesson."

Alex didn't think that was true, but he resumed walking toward the exit, a little quicker this time. Lanver called after them, and he turned. She jogged up and thrust out what seemed like a tiny bit of paper—a Band-Aid, Alex realized. He took it gratefully. "Thanks." Ripping it open, he saw that it was hot pink, with tiny Hello Kittys printed on it. "Um, do you have anything a little manlier?"

"We absolutely do," Lanver said pleasantly. With a little wave, she turned and waltzed off to the basement. Chase started laughing.

Chapter 3

By 1:00 a.m., Lindy had finished all the work that was supposed to last her the rest of the night shift, and a little of tomorrow night's work. She swung her office chair in circles, bored. Again.

This is what I get for trying to mainstream, she thought. Most shades preferred to live "off the grid" with their own kind, at least as much as was possible these days. Lindy, however, was more motivated to stay hidden than most of her so-called peers, and by now she considered herself an expert at mainstreaming. She had an apartment, a car, even a goddamned cat, not to mention a high-paying night shift job as a translator.

The problem was, she was simply too good at the work. According to her job description, Lindy was supposed to spend about forty percent of her working hours translating phone calls for the financial brokers, usually to the Japanese market, and the rest translating textual communications: e-mails, memos, financial documents, and plenty of other written materials, from instructions to travel arrangements to the occasional filthy e-mail. Unfortunately, few of the brokers bothered with phone calls anymore, and the written stuff was easy to speed through. Lindy had a serious unfair advantage: centuries of practice at languages, not to mention enhanced reflexes and concentration.

She'd learned a long time ago that it was necessary to slow herself down, lest she raise the eyebrows of her coworkers. Being good at your work is fine, but being exceptional can become extremely bad for someone whose life's mission is to blend in with humans. It was hard enough trying to hold down a human identity without raising eyebrows at your job, too. It was nearly impossible for shades to do so many simple human chores: pay taxes, own property, enter a hospital, go to the DMV, maintain a bank account. Although she could technically be out during the day, the sunlight hurt her skin, and ever since Ambrose had been captured the humans were more and more suspicious of people in ball caps and sunglasses.

Lindy stood up and paced for a bit, eyeing the desk of her officemate. Teresa worked the day shift, doing the same job. They'd shared an office for nearly five years, but had only met face to face a couple of times. The arrangement was a good way for the company to get away with giving them tiny offices, but Lindy didn't mind sharing. Sometimes when she got bored she searched Teresa's desk, telling herself she was looking for hints about how humans behaved. And it *had* provided some useful details for blending in better—Teresa had a framed picture of her cat, so Lindy brought in a framed picture of Marlowe. Teresa kept emergency tampons in her bottom drawer, so Lindy stashed away a few as well, although she hadn't menstruated in centuries. Teresa always had a bunch of dirty Tupperware around that she'd forgotten to take home and wash, so one weekend Lindy had gone to the store, bought supplies for spaghetti, and laboriously smeared it over a bunch of glass containers.

But she'd looked through Teresa's things just the night before, and there was nothing of interest. Lindy found herself glancing at her bag, where she kept her personal laptop.

It's stupid to keep fucking around on the Darknet, she reminded herself. *You don't know who could be watching.*

Resolutely, she went back to her desktop, opened a browser window, and pulled up newspapers in several languages. You were never done learning a language, because they changed and evolved every day they were used. That was why Lindy loved them. She started with the Russian newspaper first, because that was the most recent of her languages and the one she most worried about keeping up with. Then she read through the Hong Kong paper, the Tokyo paper, and three separate papers from Europe before finally switching over to *The Washington Post.* The front-page headline screamed out at her.

SHADES MURDER SEVEN MORE IN
CHICAGOLAND CORNFIELD

"Fuck!" Lindy said out loud. She spoke seven languages, but this was still the most diverse curse word, and therefore her favorite. She skimmed through the story, faster than any human speed reader. The dead agents. The single survivor, who had been nearly disemboweled by some kind of short blade. Giselle.

"Hector," she muttered under her breath. "What the fuck are you doing?"

Telling herself it was now necessary, she pulled out her personal computer and quickly flipped it open, Lindy had once drunk a world-class hacker, who'd set her up with an untraceable IP address and a little scrambler that supposedly kept her from being hacked. She remembered to turn it on despite her agitation. Her company claimed that they didn't monitor their employees' computer usage, that they trusted their own people. This, and the flexibility of their working hours, was one of the reasons Lindy had taken the position at this particular firm, instead of any of the other ones that had tried to throw money at her. Despite their promises, though, Lindy would much rather take precautions than chances.

She made her way into the Darknet and began going through the private message boards. There was no way to know how many shades there were in the world, or what percentage of them had access to the Darknet sites, but it was still the best way she knew of to gauge their opinions and moods as a group. Most of the shades—including a few she had once known personally—had posted in the last twenty-four hours to express benign concern about the murders. Nobody was reckless enough to openly speak against Hector, but they were confused: Hector himself was the one who'd adopted the stay-under-the-radar plan, figuring that if the new BPI couldn't find a single other vampire after the famous "Subject A," they would eventually decide to cut bait and go back to the way things were.

That strategy was meant to confuse the human authorities, and it was a decent plan, Lindy thought, even if it meant cutting loose that little worm, Ambrose. If the government actually got around to declaring him inhuman and torturing him, Hector would have to step in, but until then, silence was the best policy.

It was, in fact, Hector's own policy. But now he had

committed a whole series of splashy murders, and there were also a handful of shades on the message boards who were *thrilled* by the news that Hector had gone rogue. They saw the overt murders as a call to arms. Lindy knew this crowd: the ones who believed that shades were the dominant species, more evolved in every way, that they should get to do anything they wanted, blah blah blah. Lindy couldn't argue with the fact that her people were *physically* superior to humans, but they were predators. They needed a large number of prey in order to survive, and as a long-term plan, trying to "overthrow" humanity was about as silly as it got.

Meanwhile, she noted, there was no sign of Hector himself on the message boards. He was probably staying silent on purpose, to keep their people even more off balance and afraid. He was that kind of leader.

Lindy wanted to scream. He was losing the shades' trust, and undoing thousands of years worth of carefully maintained restraint. If he didn't get things back under control, or at least explain why the Chicago killings were somehow justified, they stood to lose everything. There was nothing to fear from a single human, or half a dozen humans, even armed with guns. But six billion of them? That was an enemy even Hector did not want to make.

Lindy stood up and paced. Nothing you can do about it, she told herself, walking in tight circles between her desk and Teresa's. You walked away, and it was the right decision. The *only* decision. Maybe this could be a good thing, down the road: If the BPI got more funding and resources, they could keep the shade population in check, restore the balance.

Yeah, right. They were all gonna die, the agents who went after Hector. But there was nothing she could do about it. Even if she called the BPI and warned them, what good would it do? What could she say?

But she had to do *something*.

Her computer chimed, the personal laptop, and Lindy frowned and circled the desk to check its screen. Had she set an alarm or something? The screensaver had come on, so she tapped the space bar to wake the computer up.

HELLO SIEGLIND.

She froze. The letters were enormous, taking up most of the now-black screen. *Oh, God. Please be a virus,* she thought. One of her old friends, maybe, trying to play a trick? The hope barely had time to bloom in her chest before it was extinguished.

TIME TO COME AND PLAY flashed across the screen, followed by I WILL SAVE ONE OF THEIR HEARTS FOR YOU.

Then the screen just erupted into a scrolling mess of COME AND PLAY.

COME AND PLAY.
COME AND PLAY.
COME AND PLAY.
COME AND PLAY.

Chapter 4

Lindy slammed the laptop closed and darted to the air-conditioning vent beneath her small window. She ripped the vent off its cheap old screws, uncovering the high-powered magnet she'd hidden there during her first week on the job. Lindy yanked the magnet off the metal and brought it over to the phone and computers, running it over the sides of all of them. When she was satisfied that the electronics were scrambled beyond repair, she replaced the magnet and rushed to the coat tree for her jacket. She touched her front pocket to make sure the slim wallet was in there and raced for the door without another glance at the little office.

The corridor outside her door, which had seemed perfectly normal only a moment ago, suddenly felt dark and threatening. It would be just like him to send the message and then ambush her as she ran. An obvious move, but Hector was rarely subtle. Lindy hesitated in the doorway, sniffing the air. Sure enough, someone had splashed vinegar around the room, an old shade trick for disguising scent from each another. That sealed it—she wasn't alone. Hector's people were here, waiting for her.

Something... happened... inside Lindy's nervous system, and it took her a moment to recognize the stirrings of fear. Lindy was often a little skittish around humans, concerned about giving herself away, but it had been so long since she'd felt real, tangible fear that she shivered from it. She was stronger than most of Hector's people, but he knew exactly how powerful she was, and he wouldn't send just one. *Three, at least,* she thought.

She wasn't sure what to do. Make a run for it, or hole up in her office? They were expecting her to run, which made holing up sound pretty appealing. But she knew Hector's playbook as well as he knew hers: He knew she wouldn't want any innocents harmed. Right now, this was between shades, but if she didn't come out, his people would start killing humans.

She edged through the office door, her eyes scanning the cubicles ahead. She tensed as something moved on a desk—but no, that desk was directly below a vent; it was just some papers shifting. She felt so exposed, which was undoubtedly exactly what Hector wanted. His people were always well armed; she longed for weapons. If she only had her daggers, or even a fucking crossbow. But no, she'd gotten complacent, gotten *mainstream*. It was too inconvenient to carry medieval weapons in the modern world, but now she felt like an idiot.

She crept forward, slowly, listening as hard as she could. There was a loud voice coming from Sanji's office down the hall; that was normal. The furnace, the quiet hum of the lights, a toilet flushing on the floor above her—*there*. Lindy whirled around and caught the shade who was pelting toward her at full speed, knives extended. He'd let his excitement get to him, had leapt before his comrades were in place. She slid in between his outstretched hands and grabbed his neck, using his own momentum to flip him over her own head and all the way to the ground, smashing his neck on the carpeting. *That* felt good. She left him crumpled on the floor—he'd heal in time to get out of here before sunrise, if his friends didn't collect him first—picked up his knives, and hurried down the hall. She automatically started toward the stairwell door, then stopped. They would be expecting that. Of course they would expect her to take the stairs. Lindy stepped back and retreated into the elevator instead. They wouldn't cut the cables—Hector's message said *come and play*; he wanted her alive—and even if they came in through the ceiling trapdoor they'd have to come one at a time, which was to her advantage.

Still, she was nearly vibrating with tension during the elevator ride, imagining them lining up in the lobby to burst on top of her as the elevator doors opened. She knew intellectually it wasn't possible—shades were damned fast, but only in short bursts; they weren't made to race down forty flights of stairs faster than an elevator. She held both of the knives behind her back in one hand, just to get her past the security guard. Assuming he was still alive. When the doors began to slide open she sprang out—and ran straight into a human man in a suit.

They collided hard, her forehead bumping his chin, her free hand smacking against something hard at his waist. A gun? Was he somehow working for Hector, too? Lindy reared back, faster than a human could, but the man reached out and grabbed her shoulders, steadying her. He was fast, for a human. "Ms. Frederick? Are you all right?" he asked.

The solicitous tone threw her off, as did the fact that he used her name. This guy had to be HR or maybe one of the analysts. Lindy glanced to her left and saw Drew, the night security guy, wave a hand. Drew was alive? Maybe Hector *was* trying to be subtle. She looked at the guy in front of her. "Who are you?" she demanded.

The man blinked hard. "Well, I thought we'd have a softer introduction first, but okay, sure." He flipped back one side of his suit jacket—not the side with the weapon—and pulled out a badge. Lindy's heart froze as she saw the three letters and the shield opposite them. "I'm Alex McKenna, the new special agent in charge of the Chicago BPI."

Oddly, the phrase *I was just thinking about you* bubbled up on her lips, but Lindy swallowed it down. Chicago. He'd said Chicago. She took another step backward, toward the elevator. She had a contingency plan for this—of course she did—but the computer message and the collision had thrown her off. The plan. The roof access door. But she needed to get away from this guy first. Brute force or mesmerize him?

McKenna broke in before she could decide. "Ma'am, you look like you're panicking. I just want to talk, I promise. You should know, however," he went on, "that every single exit to this building has an armed agent in front of it." He didn't sound so kind anymore. "Including the roof," he added, as though he could read her mind. His gaze flickered for a moment, and then he moved closer to her. "Ms. Frederick, I know you're a shade. I just want to talk to you," he added quietly. "You don't need the knives." Shit. He'd seen the reflection in the elevator's shiny brass.

She could mesmerize this one agent easily, but they had to have at least half a dozen. That would get messy. She thought of the shades who were no doubt prowling this building, looking for her. She had to get the agents out of there before the shades in the building decided to have some more fun with the BPI. Silently, she cursed his stupidity—didn't this guy know it was open season on government agents?

Slowly, so he could see her doing it, she brought her hand out from behind her and lowered herself far enough to drop the knives safely on the floor, feeling a tinge of disappointment. They were really nice blades. "We can talk, but not here," she said. McKenna opened his mouth to object, so she took his arm gently and propelled him back to the exit, adding, "Bring as many agents to watch us as you want, but I'm not speaking to you within a mile of this building. And if you try to make me, we'll both have a really rough night. You more than me, I bet."

A half smile flashed across his face before he composed it again. "All right," he said, nodding. "We'll take my car."

Chapter 5

Alex wasn't sure what he'd expected from Rosalind Frederick, but it wasn't a wholesome-looking blond woman with gentle curves and warm brown eyes. In her soft wraparound sweater and prim khaki pants, she was less "creature of the night" and more "hot kindergarten teacher." She did seem on edge, her eyes darting around. At first he assumed she was checking for his agents, but the woman—the *shade,* he corrected himself—didn't seem frightened of the BPI so much as just kind of . . . distracted. It was odd, but then again, this was Alex's first actual shade bust. And only the second in the history of the Bureau. Maybe they were all like Frederick.

They walked silently through the lobby, right up to the front entrance where Chase was waiting with two more agents on the outside of the door behind him. "Ms. Frederick," he said politely as they approached. His eyes met Alex's, widening with a question.

"We're going to drive around for a bit and chat," Alex explained. "Can you follow in the other car?"

Chase nodded, lifting his walkie-talkie to convey instructions to the rest of their team, on loan from the New York pod. Alex ushered Rosalind Frederick through the door, laying a hand on her upper arm as they entered the open air. The sidewalk was empty. "We do have a sharp-shooter in the building across the street," he murmured to Rosalind. "He's been dying to know if he can shoot faster than a shade can run."

She seemed unruffled. "I assure you, Agent McKenna, I have no intention of running," she replied. "You're right; we *should* talk. Just as soon as we get away from here."

Her matter-of-fact tone surprised him, but he didn't loosen his grip on her arm. If she were planning to take off, it was unlikely she'd announce it first. The town car was waiting at the curb, with one of the loaner agents behind the wheel. "Just drive around, Agent Goode," Alex instructed. He glanced at Rosalind and added, "But away from this location, please." He pressed the button to raise the privacy screen, and turned his attention to the shade beside him.

She was looking at him with some amusement. "You're not afraid to be stuck in a tiny space with me?" she said with a small smile. "I think I've been insulted."

Alex shook his head. "I've done my research on you, ma'am. My team has cross-referenced reports of assaults, murders, suspected shade attacks, and unusual disappearances near all the places where you've lived in the last twenty years. We've also talked to your neighbors and coworkers going back nearly that far. You're not violent, or at least, not as a first response."

Her expression cooled, her gaze sliding to the window as if she was checking the perimeter. "But you've backed me into a corner, haven't you? You know what they say about cornered predators. We're killers."

He grinned at her then. "Yeah, but you'll try to talk me out of it first."

Rosalind smiled back before she caught herself, and Alex knew he'd gained a small point. She smoothed her pants over her knees. "So. You say you don't want to arrest me, but you've gone to a lot of trouble to get me alone. What is it you want? Information?"

"To begin with, yes. But that's just in the short term."

"And in the long term?"

"I want to hire you."

She threw her head back and laughed, a musical sound that Alex found himself liking, even if it was at his expense. It actually took a few minutes for her giggles to subside. "You must be joking," she said, the laughter still in her voice. "Hire me to do what? Type *really* fast?"

Alex didn't smile. He just leaned forward and picked up a file from the empty passenger seat. "No. I guess you could say I need a translator. That's what you do, right?" He handed it to her. "Translate?"

"What is this?" She opened the file with a frown. Alex watched her face carefully as she flipped through the photos and documents they'd collected so far on the Chicagoland murders. Her face clouded over as she looked at the pile of bodies in the cornfield, the same shot that had caused Ambrose to freak out. She closed the file and thrust it back at him. "*Languages,* I translate languages. Not behavior. And I don't know why they're doing this. It's not . . . how we do things."

Well, he'd gotten her to admit she was a shade. That was a start, anyway. Alex leaned back in the seat. "Ms. Frederick, when I first got your name, I had every intention of going the same route with you that we went with Ambrose: locking you in a cell, observing, questioning, the whole nine yards."

"You could try," she muttered.

He let that go. "But I've been reading a lot about you. Our guys even worked up a psych profile, which is pretty much their favorite thing to do. You're on the sidelines, Ms. Frederick, and it's not an accident. You like to think of yourself as impartial, nonviolent."

Something flickered across her face, and for just a second Alex could imagine a warrior behind the soft curves and benign expression, but he pressed on. "You can't be happy about this," he said, lifting the file. "You don't want these deaths any more than I do."

She pursed her lips for a moment, as if trying to keep something behind them. Then she took a great sniff of the air, making no effort to hide it. Alex knew from the Ambrose research that she was checking his scent for shifts in pheromones, heart rate. He kept his gaze steady. "No, I don't," she said finally.

"So help me," he urged.

"From a plastic cage?"

"No. Come to Chicago with me, be on my team."

She stared at him. "Work for the BPI? You're serious? Do you realize how insane that sounds?"

"Why?"

"No one in your entire bureau will want to work with a shade."

"So we won't tell them," he replied. "I'll tell the team we suspect a language component, and you can use your current identity and everything. I'll know, one technician, and my second in command, just in case something happens to me. That will be it."

She stared at him. "You've collected a lot of data on me," she pointed out. "I'm sure you didn't do that alone. I'm guessing my current identity is already blown."

He shook his head. "As far as the research team knows, you're a suspected shade sympathizer. I've kept your status as contained as humanly possible."

She looked skeptical. "These are trained BPI agents,

Agent McKenna, not a bunch of night janitors and barflies."

"Trained agents who have never seen a shade in person, and certainly not one who looks like you," he countered. "Everyone on the team will be new, and we're going to be too busy hunting these guys for anyone to ask a lot of questions."

"Even so." She shook her head, frustrated. "You don't know what you're asking of me. You're right; I have been impartial, under the radar, and it's kept me alive. If I start telling you all about shades I'll be signing my own death warrant."

"Breaking the rules, in other words," Alex said neutrally. "There's a hierarchy, then. Interesting." Rosalind just sighed, not taking the bait, and he leaned toward her again. "Look, Ms. Frederick, it's all going to come out. I believe that, I really do. Now that we know about shades, the BPI isn't going to stop pushing until we get to dissect one. We've already begun designing weapons specifically for shades, and in a few more months Congress is going to give us permission to declare Ambrose inhuman. When that happens, it's open season on your people."

She sat quietly, just listening. "You can change all that just by working with me. Your identity is not going to come out, but even if it does, even if other shades spot you, some of them are going to see that you're working with us and it's okay. That we're treating you well, that we've found a way to coexist. And that's going to matter to them."

"You're suggesting I'll be . . . what, a mascot?" she said disdainfully.

"An example of what we could be together, shades and humans." Her expression didn't change, so he added, "Look, a few months ago, no one cared any more about shades than they did about a genocide on the other side of the world. It was compelling, sure, maybe enough to write a blog or discuss it on social media, even donate a little money. But the whole thing was too distant for anyone to actually step outside their own problems and pay attention." He gestured to the file. "These deaths in Chicago, though, they're changing that. People are starting to pay attention to shades, and all they have to see is these murders. You can help swing the balance of public opinion."

Alex had more he could say, but he could see that he'd made an impact, and he decided to quit while he was ahead. He turned his head to look out the window, giving her some time to absorb his words. Alex didn't know Cincinnati well; to him it just looked like any other city in the world: fast food places and graffitied sidewalks and homeless people. Whatever this city's cultural forte was, they weren't in it.

"Say I agree to this," came Rosalind Frederick's soft voice. "How do you know I won't run the moment you look away?"

"I've thought of that." He reached over the seat again and came up with a small container, similar to a jewelry box. "A few months ago the BPI explored the idea of releasing Ambrose with a tracker device," he explained, opening the lid. Inside was a bracelet made of linked metal, sort of like a one-inch-wide strip of chain mail. "Ultimately we decided the risks weren't worth it, but our tech team had already begun developing this tracking bracelet."

She was frowning. "Like an ankle monitor you'd give to a common parolee."

"Sure, only it costs more than I'll make in this lifetime." He picked up the bracelet, which was unusually heavy. "This is an osmium-titanium alloy. It's supposed to be unbreakable, even for shades, and once the catch fastens it requires a code to open. Of course, you could eventually get it off with the right tools, but they're not commercially available, and by the time you tracked them down we'd know."

She eyed the bracelet mistrustfully. "Look," Alex added, "it even has a little medical ID tag, so you can keep it on in situations where you'd ordinarily need to remove your jewelry."

"Very James Bond."

"It's the FBI. We have the cool toys," he said with a grin, letting her take a closer look at the bracelet.

"That's why you need a technician to know about me." She leaned back in her seat, away from the bracelet, and studied him for a long moment. Alex wondered what she saw when she looked at him—just an idealistic kid? A foolish man? Or an actual leader making a bold choice? He'd like to think of himself as the latter, but he couldn't entirely blame someone for believing something else.

"I'll give you a year," she said finally. "But I want it in writing that if I work for the BPI—as a language consultant, meaning no cage, no medical testing, nothing like that—for one year, I get immunity from any prosecution involving my . . . evolutionary status. *Permanent* immunity."

"Five years," he said. "And the agreement is null if you kill or hurt anyone."

"Two years is my absolute ceiling," she insisted, "and I can defend myself if attacked."

"Ms. Frederick—"

"Lindy."

"Lindy, how do I know you can even stop this person"—he gestured at the Chicago file, now on the seat between them—"within two years?"

"Because," she said patiently, "he's my brother."

Chapter 6

After dropping that little bombshell, Rosalind Frederick wouldn't give him any more details until she had the signed agreement from the attorney general. Alex tried and tried, even going so far as to point out that more innocent people might die before the paperwork went through, but Lindy just gave him a hard look and shook her head. She agreed to put on the tracking bracelet as a show of good faith, but she wasn't giving out any information without the paperwork in hand.

Even with Alex's new pull, getting the AG out of bed to draft a deal that would address laws that hadn't yet been put into effect would take some time. While they were waiting Alex had the driver take them to the Cincinnati FBI office, where the technician who designed the bracelet was waiting to put it on.

In a rare stroke of good luck, Noelle Liang was the star engineer at the Chicago FBI office; she had been loaned to the bracelet project and flown in specially to help with its "installation." A tall, slightly gangly Chinese American woman in her midtwenties, she was a Chicago native and had deep roots there. Chase Eddy had actually crossed paths with her before, at a seminar in D.C. He'd hit on her; she'd pointed out that her girlfriend probably wouldn't approve, and they'd struck up a casual friendship. Chase trusted her, which meant that Alex did, too. He was relieved that she'd be nearby and available for consultation during the case.

The Cincinnati lab was a meager building. The cleaning service had come and gone, but the night security guard walked them downstairs to the lab, where Noelle was the only occupant. Chase walked in with them and introduced Noelle, who wore a miniskirt and a T-shirt with the periodic table underneath her white lab coat. It was nearly three in the morning, but she looked peppy and excited, like a little kid about to debut a new stock car. She shook Lindy's hand enthusiastically, but Alex didn't miss the little gleam of "I want to study you" in her eyes, and he doubted Lindy did, either. "Love this clandestine nighttime shit," she said, leading them to a lab table with two stools, a bright light, and a set of tools that looked more appropriate for a watchmaker than an FBI lab tech. Noelle climbed on one stool and motioned for Lindy to take the other. "You've got my bracelet?" she asked Alex.

He handed it over. "You made the modification I asked for, right?"

She gave him a look of mock injury. "Of course I did."

"Modification?" Lindy said pointedly.

"Yeah." Noelle picked up the bracelet and flipped it over with one hand, pushing her purple-streaked hair behind her ear with the other. There was a small metal square on the back, roughly the size of a nickel. "This is the casing for the tracking device." She pointed to an indentation where a second casing had been removed. "This used to be a second device, sort of a teeny little Taser controlled by remote. When we were gonna put it on a hostile we wanted to be able to zap him with a couple hundred thousand volts. Alex had me remove it for you."

"And he wanted the brownie points for doing it, which is why he brought it up just now," she said, sounding unimpressed.

Alex shrugged. "I'm playing it straight with you, Lindy. You need to know that."

Lindy nodded and told Noelle to go ahead. The engineer picked up a few of the tiny tools and fiddled with the complex latch for a few minutes until it was secure. Then she put the tools back on the tray in precise order. "Damn, I'm good," she said admiringly. To Lindy, Noelle added, "Do me a favor? Try to rip it off? But, like, *really* try."

Lindy gave the bracelet a cursory tug, and then at

Noelle's encouraging look, she braced her back against the side of the lab table and *pulled*. The bracelet gave the tiniest creak, but held fast. The shade looked impressed, and Noelle and Chase high-fived.

"If something happens to these two," Lindy said, tilting her head at Alex and Chase, "will you be able to take it off as well?"

Noelle nodded. "Actually, for the next two years, I'll be the only one with the code. This is to prevent you from, um . . ." She glanced uneasily at the two male agents.

Lindy gave her a bemused look. "Spitting in their drinks and making them give it to me?"

"Well . . . yeah. I'll be working in a different department, different building, and my understanding is that someone from the Chicago pod will be with you most of the time. . . ." She shrugged.

"This system isn't designed to be perfect," Alex broke in. "It's designed to communicate our guarded trust in you. I'm really hoping you'll feel like we deserve the same respect."

Lindy just gave him a thoughtful look.

At that moment Alex's cell phone rang, and he stepped a few feet away to answer it. When he returned, there was a new energy to his step. "You've got your agreement," he told Lindy. "The AG just sent it to your attorney's office. Is it safe to assume she keeps night hours?"

Lindy rolled her eyes at him and dug out her own phone, the metal bracelet jingling on her wrist. She shot Alex an accusatory glare. "Is this like putting a bell on a cat?"

Noelle winced. "Sorry," she said, looking truly apologetic. "That metal alloy is rare and difficult to work with, but I'll start looking for a way to muffle the noise."

Lindy called her lawyer, and they spent the next few hours dealing with the formalities of Lindy's deal and getting Alex, Chase, and Lindy booked on the 5 a.m. flight to Chicago. Noelle wanted to return to her hotel for a few hours of sleep before catching a later flight during the day. She wished them luck.

Alex offered to stop by Lindy's apartment so she could pack some things, but she demurred, saying she'd prefer that a BPI agent just stop there during daytime hours and get a suitcase and her cat. The only reasoning she gave was "so we don't wake the neighbors." Alex didn't really understand, but the more he questioned it, the more distant she got, so he just shrugged and relayed the order. Lindy spent the rest of the ride scribbling out a list of items for the agent to grab.

There was no security line at the airport, but they did lose a little time when the TSA agent had questions about Lindy's medical alert bracelet. Alex eventually just flashed his badge and said Lindy had a rare blood disease. The TSA agent looked her up and down, shrugged, and waved them through.

When they were finally seated on the plane, Lindy asked for the aisle seat, then reached across Alex to carefully lower the window shade. It was still dark outside, but the sun would be coming up during the three-hour flight.

"So the sun allergy thing is real then," Alex said conversationally. "We suspected as much, since Ambrose seems to react to sunlight, but a few agents thought he was faking it."

"No, it's real." She shrugged and amended, "Well, sort of. We are much weaker when the sun is out—generally we slow down to human speed, human everything. And if I were left in a desert all day with no shade, it would kill me by nightfall. But ducking in and out, sticking to the shadows, we can survive just fine during the day. I suspect that's where the name came from."

Alex looked disappointed. "Aw, so you don't explode into dust?"

She laughed. "Would I have gotten on a plane with you if I did? No, you should assume that most of the vampire legends you've heard are bullshit. Most of them were rumors started by us, in fact."

Alex couldn't help a yawn, then—a big one. He'd been awake for a long time. She smiled, and he returned it with visible embarrassment. "Sorry. Do you sleep?" he asked her. "Ambrose seems to, but our people think he might be faking."

"Eventually. We usually catch a couple of hours right after sunrise, just to give our muscles and skin a chance to recuperate," she replied offhandedly. "We can go days without it, though, if we need to."

The plane began to fill up, and Alex was conscious of the civilians moving past them: harried mothers, cranky toddlers, older men with briefcases. He wished they hadn't needed to fly commercial—he had about a thousand questions for this woman, but he wasn't stupid enough to say anything that might give her away, not in front of the arriving passengers. The wall separating them from first-class was directly in front of them, and the BPI had managed to buy out the row directly behind them, where Chase was already snoring against the window. But there were still far too many people moving past.

So he watched Lindy quietly, marveling at how human she seemed. Even after meeting Ambrose—maybe especially after meeting Ambrose—he had considered shades an Other. Not a thing, exactly—he wasn't one of *those* people—but the way he'd reacted to Alex's blood . . . it was like hanging out with a mountain gorilla.

Lindy was a different story. She looked harmless, of course, but she also had regular human manner-isms—checking her lipstick in a compact mirror, jiggling a leg when she was impatient, even flipping through the in-flight magazine during the flight attendant's safety speech. And she was undeniably attractive. If he'd stopped to really consider what a female shade would look like, Alex would have pictured a stereotypical badass: all muscles, dangerous glares, and leather from head to toe. Lindy, on the other hand, looked as if she spent her weekends chaperoning church camp. She twirled a strand of hair around one finger while she was reading, for Christ's sake. He couldn't think of her as a shade at all, just a woman.

Which probably made her far more dangerous than Ambrose, he reminded himself, with or without the plex-iglass cell.

Chapter 7

Agent McKenna was quiet for the first part of the flight, just giving her the occasional sideways glance. He was a fidgety man: cracking his knuckles and shifting his position, as if maybe if he just squirmed around enough he could make his body believe it was in motion. When the seatbelt sign went off and the rest of the plane settled into a low murmur, Lindy could practically see him start to salivate. "Are you ready to tell me about that brother comment?" he asked quietly.

Lindy closed the crappy in-flight magazine and sighed, checking her watch. "Twenty whole minutes. I never thought you'd make it this long."

McKenna didn't smile. "You're going to have to trust me with this eventually," Alex pointed out, "if you're going to help me put him away."

His tone felt sanctimonious to her, and she whipped her head around to look at him. "Another trophy for Camp Vamp?" she spat.

"If he makes it that far," Alex said levelly. "A guy kills this many people, I can't really see him going quietly."

The anger drained from Lindy as quickly as it had arrived. "No." She closed her eyes for a moment, unable to push aside the sudden image of Hector as a smiling, golden-haired child, helping her steal buns from the kitchen maids. "He won't."

She knew her tone was still guarded, and McKenna seemed to pick up on the reluctance. He glanced around for a second to make sure no one was looking at them, and then passed her a worn manila folder. "Why don't you look this over?" he said quietly. "I showed you some photos before, but this is everything we have on the missing kids case."

She recognized the manipulation but nodded and accepted the file, the tracking bracelet jingling on her wrist. Glancing around to make sure no one was paying any attention to her, Lindy flipped open the file and started reading from the beginning.

Most of the information she saw had been published in the newspapers: the names of the seven missing teens and the small towns where they'd vanished. All seven lived within about an hour's drive from Chicago, but there was no other discernible pattern. Five of the seven were still in high school, and their experiences varied widely: a cheerleader, an overweight tuba player, a valedictorian-elect. The remaining two had graduated high school but stayed at home: Ethan Harrison had no college prospects and had kept working at his dad's farm, and Chloe Davis, the girl taken the night of the botched raid, had been accepted to Northwestern but deferred for a year to save up some money.

In her head, Lindy cursed at Hector in every language she knew. When she'd read the whole thing, Lindy passed the file back to Alex.

"Okay," she said wearily. "What do you want to know?"

"Let's start with how you know it's him," McKenna suggested.

She wasn't ready to tell him about Hector finding her online, and couldn't see how it would be helpful, anyway, so Lindy said, "I've suspected for a while, but I knew for sure when you showed me the photos in the car. The pile of bodies, that's Giselle's signature move. And Giselle works for my brother."

McKenna nodded approvingly, as if she'd passed a test. "Did anything in the complete file stand out?"

"A few things." She ticked them off on her fingers. "First, the ages. He wants teenagers because they're easier to manipulate than adults. I'm guessing most of these kids weren't taken, exactly—they willingly left with Giselle or Hector or one of his people, maybe without even being mesmerized." Alex nodded. "Except for Bobbi Klay," she went on. "A tiny percentage of humans are fairly immune to shade saliva, just as a tiny percent are incredibly susceptible to mesmerization."

Alex was surprised. He took out a small notebook and started scribbling. "That's interesting. You think Bobbi Klay was one of these?"

"I do. When they couldn't control her they decided to cut their losses and use her as a food source." As soon as the words were out of her mouth she realized they had come out too cold, too *vampire*. It showed on Alex's face. "Sorry," she added quickly. "I didn't mean to be callous. I'm impressed with Bobbi, really. She was a fighter, and she deserved better."

He nodded, accepting the apology. "Okay, that's good to know. What else?"

She ticked off another finger. "Second, no one else has mentioned that Sophie Allman and Chloe Davis are cousins."

He shrugged. "It's a tenuous connection: Allman's father and Davis's mother are estranged, and they live nearly two hours apart. The girls had only met a few times."

She thought that over for a moment, and asked, "Are there any other connections between the missing kids?"

"No, why? What's he doing with them?"

"I don't know for sure, but I assume he's transmuting them."

Alex nodded. "Our profilers suggested as much. But to what end? Is he creating an army? Planning some big infection?"

"I don't *know*," she said, sounding as frustrated as he felt. "You don't get it: When I said this isn't how we do things, I meant it." She shook her head. "Even centuries ago, when our existence was just sort of generally accepted by the human public, taking a lot of people from the same area, this close together, was never something shades did. It was considered . . . uncouth. And too high profile. It'd be like a human hunter walking into a zoo with a rifle and shooting a buffalo, then dragging it home. If a shade wants to make a new fledgling, there are far subtler ways."

"Were you around back then?"

She didn't respond. In her long, long life, Lindy had told very few humans what she was. The ones who did find out, however, always wanted to know her age. By now she knew better than to give it.

"Okay, fine." Alex shifted in his seat, and to her surprise, he added, "Maybe that was a rude question. Maybe when you get to know me a little better, you'll trust me with the answer. Fair enough?"

She nodded.

"Meanwhile, what else can you tell me about your brother?"

"Hector," she said softly. "His name is Hector."

McKenna gave her a brisk nod. "Thank you for that. Last name?"

"No idea what he's using now. It doesn't matter, really; he won't be mainstreaming, like I was. He'll be way off the grid." She gestured at the file. "My guess is he's in a rural area outside Chicago. He'd need space and privacy to transmute the teenagers."

Frown. "Tell me about that process, please."

Lindy glanced around again, but no one was paying any attention. "Transmuting someone is very difficult," she said in a low voice. "The process involves bleeding the person out and inserting saliva into their heart. The heart itself, not just the bloodstream. In the past, this could get very . . . messy. Nowadays it can be done with syringes."

"Okay." He was scribbling notes again, so she paused for a second to let him catch up before continuing.

"But shades of a certain age can take it a step further." She reached out—he managed not to flinch—and touched his tie, right over his heart. "If I put my *blood* in there, too, I can create a connection that goes deeper even than the elder-fledgling bond. I can talk to you. In your head. And know where you are at all times, within about . . . oh, a city block."

His pen went still, and when he looked up there was

shock all over his face. "You're talking about telepathy."

She nodded. "But it's one way only. The theory is that this ability developed so an elder could give his fledgling orders in battle."

"That's . . . we didn't know that." His eyes went distant for a moment. "Someone could be talking to Ambrose? Or Ambrose could be talking to someone else?"

Lindy hesitated. Did she want to reveal her connection to the captured shade? No, she didn't want McKenna drawing any kind of similarity between her and that little worm. He must have been the one who had given McKenna Lindy's name, which meant Hector had Lindy's current name and had told his pet sycophant. But why would Ambrose give it to the BPI, when Hector already had people after her? Unless Ambrose had done it without Hector's permission. *That* would be interesting.

"In theory," she said finally.

He eyed her with sudden interest. "Does your elder send *you* messages?"

The memory was like an assault: her father, with blood on his mouth and his tunic, screaming at them to run. "My elder is dead now," she said shortly.

"Do you have . . . um . . . fledglings?"

"Not anymore." Her tone made it clear that she didn't want to discuss it any further, and McKenna was still trying to win her over—he didn't push. She respected him for that, and it made her next decision a little easier. She pushed out a breath she didn't need to take. "Look, Agent McKenna—"

He gave her the quarterback grin again. "You can call me Alex."

Goddamn it, she didn't mean to smile back at him. "Alex. There's something you need to know about Hector and me, and I need you to not freak out."

That scared him a little, she could see, and he tried to cover it with bluster. "You're not gonna tell me there's a *Game of Thrones*–style incest thing happening there, are you?"

Lindy snorted. She was tempted to mess with him on that, but no, this was too important. "No. Our relationship is intense, for siblings, but not sexual. But I said that the telepathy was one way only. That's not always true. There are cases of shades with a common elder who can communicate mentally with each other, and also respond to their elder. It's only possible with relatives, with a very close blood connection. Twins, for example."

Alex's eyes widened, and she heard his pulse speed up. "You and Hector? You can talk to each other?" He probably wasn't even aware that his hand was going to his gun.

Gently, she put a hand on his forearm. "I can hear your pulse racing. I need you to calm down."

"If you're sending him thoughts right now, and reading his—" The stark professionalism was back in his voice, and he looked ready to arrest her right there on the plane.

"It doesn't work like that. I . . . underwent a procedure."

"What procedure?"

"Every few years, I have to have a complete transfusion." She wrinkled her nose. "When I say *complete,* I mean that every drop of blood is drained from my body and replaced with someone else's—blood that has no connection to my brother's."

"Someone must help you with that."

She nodded. "But I won't tell you who. What you need to know is that Hector can't send me thoughts, and I can't send him mine. But he can still sense when I'm close."

His hand eased off his gun as he began to relax. "How close? Will he be able to find you?"

She shook her head. "Not exactly, no. But he'll feel me enter his territory. He'll know I'm around, without being able to pinpoint it exactly."

Alex asked a number of follow-up questions about how the location finding worked and why. She couldn't answer him. Modern science was able to explain a lot about shades already, but there were some things that were beyond it yet—especially considering the smartest scientific minds in the world had only known about shades for a less than two years. No time at all, really. Finally, Alex got around to the obvious question. "Why did you cut yourself off from your brother?"

She considered the question. She hadn't lied to Alex McKenna yet, but how could she sum up more than a millennia of history between two people? It was impossible, and although she knew she would have to give Alex McKenna a better understanding of shades, she wasn't entirely comfortable letting him in on their history. Or her place in it.

"We had a difference of opinion," she said at last, "about thirty years ago. Since then, he's tried to find me, and I've tried to stay away from him."

"Will you tell me what you two fought over?"

His voice was gentle, compassionate even, but Lindy wasn't a fool. "Not unless it could save lives," she stated.

Alex scribbled a few more notes, and they sat in companionable silence for a while. Behind them, Chase Eddy let out a loud snore, and Lindy and Alex exchanged a smile.

"He has sinus problems," Alex said apologetically. "I keep telling him to have the surgery, but he thinks everyone will make fun of him."

"You guys are close, I take it." It had been written

all over their body language and even their scents—not sex, but the kind of bond that came with sharing clothes, sharing spaces, eating the same foods and drinking the same drinks.

Alex nodded, looking a little guilty. "He's been my best friend since college. He's coming to Chicago to watch my back."

Lindy felt a pang of wistfulness. It had been a long time since someone had "watched her back." She could hardly remember what it was like.

The pilot announced their descent into Chicago, and the seatbelt lights went on. Alex started to raise his seat tray. "Tell me about what happens when we land," Lindy suggested.

"We'll go straight from O'Hare to the hotel where we're all staying. The Bureau is putting us up for a month, or until we find new homes, whichever comes first," he said. "We'll get a couple of hours to shower and sleep, and be at the BPI headquarters at 10 a.m. for a briefing. The rest of the team will meet us there, with the exception of Ruiz, who's still in the hospital."

Lindy bit her lip. "It's interesting to me that they left one alive," she said.

"How do you mean?"

She shrugged. "Giselle . . . she's a sociopath. She does anything Hector wants, but she's in it for the fun. That's what she thinks killing is: fun. I'd keep an eye on this Ruiz guy. Giselle is like a cat with a whole nest of mice: She might be saving him to play with later."

He nodded. "I was gonna call the hospital to check on him this morning anyway. I'll send a message to add to the guard on his door."

He pulled out a cell phone and fiddled with it, turning it back on and putting it to his ear. Lindy reminded herself that she was going to need a new one of those soon. She started to mention it to him, but he put up a finger. "Hang on, I have voice mail." He listened, frowning, then leaned over to wake up Agent Eddy. The agent behind them woke up with a start and leaned forward to put his face near the crack between their seats. "There was a development overnight," Alex said quietly.

"Another missing kid?" Eddy asked.

The SAC shook his head. "They found two of the bodies in a culvert outside of Heavenly. About twenty minutes ago."

"How long have they been dead?" Eddy asked immediately.

McKenna's face was expressionless. "ME says about six hours."

Chapter 8

When the call came on Monday morning, Ruiz was awake, flipping channels on his hospital room television. He would only accept the bare minimum of morphine, and that was only because the pain was too intense for him to think without it. The goddamned vampire had very nearly disemboweled him, and after a day and a half in surgery he had twenty staples and sixty stitches, inside and out, holding his guts in. Since then he'd slept only when his body's exhaustion finally overcame the pain, but it always woke him up again within a few hours.

The call came from Sarah Greer, the Chicago BPI's office manager. Sarah was a no-nonsense, slightly brusque woman in her late forties or early fifties, and she had a soft spot for Ruiz. They both told it like it was, she'd said once. Like most of the surviving BPI staff, Sarah had dropped by to see him on his first day in the hospital, but unlike the others, who'd left after a cursory visit, she returned the next day with homemade cookies and a stack of cheap paperbacks. She was good people, and unlike most of his well-wishers, Ruiz was pleased to see her name on the caller ID.

"Hey, Sarah," he croaked. His voice was hoarse with disuse, because speaking consumed energy he didn't have. "What's going on?"

"Agent Ruiz," Greer said, and he recognized the heaviness in her voice. *Someone's dead.* Of course. He felt stupid: Why else would she be calling this early? "The sheriff's department in Heavenly recovered two of the kids' bodies this morning. I thought you'd want to know."

He blinked, pushing the button on his hospital bed to make himself sit up. He hadn't expected to recover any more bodies. He'd expected to encounter several new shades. "Which ones?"

"Budchen and Harrison."

Two of the earlier victims, taken nearly two months ago. Ruiz cursed. Rachel Budchen was the youngest of the missing kids, just sixteen years old. She was a cheerleader who didn't do so well in school, but her grades had recently begun an upswing after a concerned teacher discovered Rachel's dyslexia. She didn't deserve to die, and neither did Ethan Harrison. "Where?" Ruiz growled.

"Don't you start," Greer said severely. "You can't go out there. This was just a courtesy call; you're supposed to be in the hospital for at least another ten days."

"Wouldn't dream of it," Ruiz said. "But I'm just sitting here staring at the ceiling; I might as well think about the case. Where did they dump 'em?"

Greer paused for a second, deciding whether to trust him. Finally she said, "The big culvert on I-43, just out of town."

As soon as he was off the phone, Ruiz began disconnecting the machines.

～

There was a portable plastic tent erected around the crime scene—standard Bureau procedure. That meant someone from the BPI was already here, Ruiz realized. He doubted the Heavenly sheriff had sophisticated evidence-gathering tools. The area in front of the tent was cordoned off with the traditional yellow tape, but a crowd of onlookers was gathered around it, whispering to one another and shouting the occasional remark at the sheriff's deputy guarding the barrier. Ruiz slowly, painstakingly pushed his way through these people, staggering like an extra in a zombie movie, one hand locked across his stitches to keep them from being jarred too much. At the crime scene tape, Ruiz held his badge up to the sheriff's deputy, who nodded and let him amble past with awe in his eyes. Ruiz had been on the front page of the Heavenly weekly newspaper the day before.

When he reached the entrance Ruiz had to pause and deal with the problem of getting the tent flap up. It lifted diagonally, and there was just no way he'd be able to raise his arm that high. He stood there for a long moment, feeling stupid, until the baby deputy guarding the line realized the problem and hustled over to lift the flap. Ruiz grunted his thanks.

There were five people inside—well, five living ones: the sheriff, the same two FBI techs who'd been helping with the rest of the investigation, and two people Ruiz didn't recognize. Every single one of them stopped what they were doing and stared in silent shock as Ruiz approached. Finally, one of the new people—a kid in a rumpled suit—stepped forward. "Agent Ruiz. I'm Special Agent in Charge Alex McKenna." He extended a hand, which Ruiz just stared at. Eventually the kid realized why Ruiz couldn't shake and stepped back again, mumbling an apology. He gestured to the woman beside him. "This is Lindy Frederick. She's a consultant working with the BPI on these murders."

A consultant? That was new. Ruiz studied her. She didn't look like a federal agent, that was for sure. Frederick was doe-eyed and curvy—not overweight, Ruiz thought, just a little fuller in the hips and bust than most of the gym-toned female agents he'd met. She wore a BPI baseball cap and Windbreaker over jeans, despite the warm morning, and she looked tired and drawn—although Ruiz certainly must have looked a hell of a lot worse. He would have dismissed her as an inconsequential lightweight, a temporary hire who would bail as soon as it got bloody, except there was something about her he couldn't quite put a finger on. Then Ruiz realized that unlike the sheriff or even the techs, Frederick didn't look the least bit repulsed or disgusted by the bodies behind her. She just looked . . .

Annoyed? No: frustrated. Like you'd look at a dog that just wouldn't stop peeing on your rug.

Ruiz just nodded at both of them, because if he was being honest, the thought of speaking and standing at the same time made him nauseous. He shuffled forward to see around the two new people. Behind them, the two teens had been tossed in a crumpled heap, with Budchen lying half on top of Harrison. Both of them were naked.

"What are you doing out of the hospital, Agent Ruiz?" McKenna asked, a clumsy attempt to gain control of the situation. "My information suggested you would need twenty-four-hour care for a couple of weeks yet. I was planning to stop in this afternoon and introduce myself."

"Just a day pass," Ruiz said in a mumble. Best he could do. "Got a cab waiting to take me back. On my own dime," he added, in case McKenna wanted to raise a stink. "Why haven't they been covered?"

McKenna looked ready to protest for a moment, but then shrugged, letting it go. "The local sheriff's office asked us to do evidence collection. I called in an FBI team, but they arrived about three minutes ago. We're working on it."

Ruiz nodded and moved closer. Now that he was almost on top of the bodies, he saw that they were very different: Budchen didn't appear to have a mark on her, other than a few bruises at her wrists and ankles. Restraint marks. The other kid, Harrison, had been ripped open, literally: sliced down the middle, his ribcage cracked wide like a walnut shell. There was no blood at all, but Ruiz could see ruptured organs peeking out through the opening. He swallowed hard, trying to keep his gorge down. There was already some vomit in the corner of the tent, and the smell hit his nostrils just as he was trying to control his stomach. He swayed on his feet. Most of the people in the tent moved forward, but it was the consultant, Frederick, who took a few quick steps to his side, holding his elbow. She was strong under those curves, and he let a little of his weight sag onto her. He shot her a grateful look. The sheriff and his deputy made an excuse about getting some fresh air and stepped out of the tent, leaving the three BPI employees alone.

No one spoke for a long moment, and Ruiz had time to look around the dank culvert opening. It hadn't rained in over a week, so the ground near the kids was fairly dry, which ruled out the possibility of them floating here from somewhere else. "Why dump them here?" he asked aloud. "They've never gone back to the same town before. Even Klay was dumped in a new location."

"They're getting bolder," McKenna remarked. "They think we can't catch them, and so far they've been right."

"More than that," Frederick said quietly. "Even a shade would want to use a car to transport dead bodies, and the longer you're in a car with the dead, the better the chances you'll get stopped or pulled over. I think wherever their base of operations is, it's not too far from here."

Ruiz gave her a look. "Who are you again?" he asked. It came out more confrontational than he'd intended, and he tried to amend it with, "I mean, why are you here?" Nope, that sounded even worse. The painkillers were not helping his already crappy manners.

She gave him an oblique look. "I'm a language and communication specialist. I've been studying the shades as a personal project, and contacted Agent McKenna in that regard. He offered me a job."

Ruiz grunted. He didn't like the idea of a civilian on the BPI team, but hey, what were the odds that any of them were going to survive the week, anyway? "You know why they were treated so different?" he asked, nodding at the bodies.

"I may have an idea—" she began, but at that moment Ruiz's knees gave out, and he started to crumple. Frederick actually held his weight for a second, but then she, too, began to buckle, and McKenna rushed forward.

"That's enough," said the new SAC firmly. "Ruiz, you've seen everything there is to see here. I'm ordering you back to your hospital bed, and if you don't go now I'll suspend you."

Ruiz glared at him, but he could barely get the breath to protest. He'd known the second he pulled the IV that he'd be working on borrowed time, and it had just run out. McKenna saw his concession and began to back up to help him out of the tent, but Ruiz summoned the fragments of his willpower and pulled himself upright. He was about to insist that he'd walk out by himself, but then he saw the opportunity he'd be passing up. "Miss Frederick, you mind walking me back to the cab?" he said to the attractive young woman, doing his best to look contrite.

She blinked in surprise but answered, "Well, of course. And please call me Lindy."

He grunted. She returned to her position under his shoulder and edged him back through the tent flap, past the group of anxious onlookers and the journalists who were beginning to arrive. Ruiz kept his head down, hoping he wouldn't be recognized. In their rush to get to the carnage, the reporters barely give him a glance, probably taking him for some old fool who got a little faint after getting a glimpse of the corpses. Let 'em.

The cab was still thirty feet ahead, idling in the road, and Ruiz finally saw his chance. "What's your theory?" he muttered to the young woman.

She gave him a sidelong glance but actually answered. "I think he's experimenting with them. Trying to change them."

"Like, he doesn't know how to make a new shade? How is that possible?"

"That's not what I mean. . . . Look, you don't seem so good, health-wise. Why don't we have this conversation when you're feeling a little better?"

He made an effort to straighten up, take some of the weight off her. "Or we can just talk now," he said firmly, stopping in front of the cab.

She rubbed her lower lip for a second, thinking it over, then reached out and took his hand. "Listen, Agent Ruiz, don't you think the best thing for you to do would be to go back to the hospital, get some good, solid rest, and worry about this later?"

Suddenly, Ruiz felt a little foolish. Of course that was the best thing to do. Rest, that was what he really needed. He could think more about all of this after he'd had some good rest. Feeling suddenly very tired, he thanked Lindy and climbed into the cab.

Chapter 9

Lindy did feel a little bad about mesmerizing Ruiz, but it was for the man's own good. To assuage her guilt, she gave the cab driver a hundred-dollar bill to cover the fare, and Ruiz was too out of it to protest. When the cab was nothing but a dust cloud on the dirt road leading to the culvert, she turned back to the tent, squinting against the sun. The hat and long-sleeved Windbreaker that Alex McKenna had offered her made it bearable, but she still felt exposed and vulnerable. She was always exposed and vulnerable during the day, really, but it also gave her a kind of safety: There wouldn't be any other shades out here to spot her. Most of them were too young to be out like this; they stayed inside.

She stepped back over to the tent and watched the buzz of activity around her. In all her many lives, Lindy had seen plenty of crime scenes, even caused some of them herself. She'd never experienced it from the police side of things, however. The BPI had taken over the crime scene now, using one of the FBI's veteran evidence collection teams. Lindy trailed Alex McKenna, watching as he oversaw the *procedure* of it all: There was a certain way for everything to be bagged, documented, studied, put away. There was a rhythm to conducting interviews, interacting with the local police, keeping the onlookers away from the crime scene, talking to reporters. It was a lot like on television, actually, except for the FBI veterans there was a banality here, a long unraveling of time as everyone trudged through the motions. Meanwhile, behind the federal team, the local law enforcement officers ran crowd control, watching the agents with wide, excited eyes.

Although the procedure of collecting information was interesting, unfortunately there was very little information to be had. No one had seen or heard the vehicle that dropped off the two corpses. The physical evidence confirmed that the bodies had been moved, but immediate results didn't give any indication of where the kids had been killed.

The kids. Lindy had been alive too long to be hurt by the deaths of strangers, but she could still get upset about waste, and that's what this was: wasted potential. These teenagers could have gone on to become anything, up to and including shades themselves, but instead Hector had just tossed them away. Looking around at the grief-stricken, angry faces crowding the yellow crime scene tape, Lindy realized that each stolen life was a rock dropped into a pond of grief, sending ripples and waves that would affect this entire community for years. And for what? For *nothing*. It was disgraceful.

It was afternoon when Alex and Chase finally finished at the crime scene, and the SAC announced that they would go back to the hotel in Chicago for a few hours of rest before convening with the new team members and making a plan. Lindy had expected him to want to start hashing it out in the rental car, or at least ask her more questions, but no, the two male agents were subdued on the ride back, their thoughts tainted by the death of the young. Lindy understood that seeing the dead teens had made this whole thing real for them: not an abstraction, not a puzzle to solve. She kept quiet.

The hotel was a generic chain in the suburb closest to Bureau headquarters, probably the best the government could afford. Lindy's suitcase and her cat wouldn't arrive until late in the day, so there was nothing for her to un-pack, nothing for her to do. She considered reading the files again or maybe catching a couple of hours of rest, but she was too wound up after seeing the wasted bodies. So she shed the BPI Windbreaker and cap, put on a Cubs hoodie she'd bought at the airport, and pocketed the new cell phone that McKenna had had sent to her room. Then she walked to the nearest train station.

While the rest of the team slept, Lindy walked

Chicago, a city she had once loved. Lindy had spent a few years here in the early twentieth century, curious about Chicago's unusual circumstances. Big cities usually began in one spot and sprawled out or up, but most of Chicago had burned to the ground in 1871. When the city planners began to rebuild, they did it with an emphasis not on speed or necessity but on architecture and beauty. Lindy had fallen in love with the city that rose from the ashes, and she had been back to visit several more times, the last in 1980. It was wonderful to walk the streets again, with reality layered over her own memories. The city had changed in a lot of the ways she'd expected—a Starbucks on every corner, fewer overt drug dealers and prostitutes, more and more vagrants—but also in ways she hadn't. Everyone now walked the streets wearing headphones and staring at their little glowing screens, for one thing. There were signs advertising street festivals and outdoor jazz concerts, monuments honoring not just presidents and national figures, but local heroes and athletes. Despite the oblivious residents, there was a sense of pride now, of community, not just for different bands of immigrants, as she remembered, but for individual neighborhoods, interests, types of music. For someone who had spent hundreds of years observing human behavior, it was fascinating to see.

Of course, in addition to re-familiarizing herself with

the city, she intended to see what would happen if she went just a little bit AWOL. She hadn't told McKenna or Chase she was planning an outing, and she half expected to catch one of the BPI staff trailing behind her, perhaps holding a GPS device tracking the bracelet's progress. At the very least, she expected to get a call on the cell phone, though she didn't even know its number yet. But to her pleasant surprise, Alex seemed true to his word about giving her some space. Oh, surely someone was sitting at a screen at FBI headquarters watching her movements as a little dot on a screen, but she appreciated even the semblance of freedom. It made her feel a little lighter, and made the bracelet feel much less like a handcuff.

~

In the hospital room, the exhaustion of healing finally overtook Ruiz, and he fell into a deep sleep, a light snore escaping through his open mouth in the hospital bed. From the window, Giselle smiled happily. *About fucking time*, she thought. She was actually impressed with this specimen: Not only had he survived her knife wounds, but according to his daytime nurse, he'd actually pulled out his IV this morning and gone to see where Giselle had left the failures. The nurse was still livid about it, even after a heavy dose of vampire saliva. Ruiz had willpower, or maybe just extreme stubbornness. It was so rare in the humans these days. He would make a lovely pet.

She tilted her head as she watched him sleep, studying him. After a moment of snoring, Giselle rapped her knuckles lightly on the window. Nothing. Excellent. There was a guard in front of his door in the hospital, but the specimen's room was on the sixth floor. They thought the height would keep her away, apparently, which was just adorable. The window itself was four feet wide and only about ten inches tall, but that was more than Giselle needed, even in the daytime. Crouching on the windowsill, she opened the small backpack and got out her burglar tools, carving a small hole in the glass and reaching a hand in to open the window. Giselle wasn't a fan of this cloak-and-dagger bullshit—she'd much rather have kicked in the whole thing—but though she could be reckless, she wasn't stupid. The situation called for subtlety.

When the long window was open, Giselle effortlessly flipped into a plank position and slid her upper half in, executing a graceful roll on the carpet and coming up on the balls of her feet. She'd half expected Ruiz to be pointing a gun at her forehead when she rose, but no, that was expecting too much of her feisty little pet. She blew him a kiss and started toward the IV stand. On the way she let her fingers trace along the covers, and when he didn't stir she walked her index finger and middle finger lightly up his leg. He remained still, but on a whim, she gave his groin a honk. *That* got his attention. Ruiz's eyes jolted open, and in one quick move Giselle vaulted herself onto the bed so she was straddling his chest above his wounds. As he drew breath to scream she ducked down and kissed him, jamming her tongue in his mouth. He stiffened, then his whole body relaxed as the saliva hit his system. Giselle sat up.

"There," she said, satisfied. Even during the daylight, at her weakest, this was too easy. "You're going to be very, very quiet, aren't you?"

Ruiz's eyes had already dulled, and he nodded eagerly. Usually it took her victims a few more seconds to look at her with that kind of devotion. *Interesting.* "Good boy!" she said approvingly. She flipped herself off him, standing beside the bed, and pulled back the sheet to expose his bandages. She pulled those off, too, squealing with pleasure at the long line of stitches. "Look at that! My best work, I think." Looking back up at his face, she added, "Forgive me, darling. I shouldn't have, but I *so* wanted to see what your insides looked like. I just couldn't resist." She held up her hands, making wiggly motions with her fingers. "All those slimy little pieces working so hard to keep you alive! It's funny every time." She flipped the bandages down and pulled the sheet over him again. "Now," she said, pulling the prepared syringe out of her bag, "let's have a bit more fun, shall we?"

Ruiz nodded eagerly. His lips parted, as if to speak, but no sound came out through the haze of painkillers and shade saliva. Giselle frowned. "That won't do," she complained. "How can you answer my questions if you can't talk?" To her amusement, he struggled to answer the question, but achieved nothing more than a few grunts. Giselle patted his chest with one hand and held up the syringe with the other. "There, there. I've got the solution. Literally." She inserted the needle into his IV port and pushed through the clear liquid. Within seconds, Ruiz's already dulled eyes began to glaze over. Giselle looked down at the stitches. After a few moments, the flesh began to knit together. She never grew tired of watching that.

"Now, before we get to playtime, I have some questions about those bodies you found today. Who came from the BPI? What were their names?"

"McKenna," Ruiz grunted. "Eddy." Giselle nodded encouragingly. They already knew about McKenna and Eddy from the mole inside the so-called Camp Vamp facility. Ruiz paused, straining to remember. "And a woman. Frederick."

"Frederick?" Giselle frowned. Wasn't that the name Sieglind had been using in Cincinnati? "Was she in chains? Handcuffs?"

"Naw. She was just walking around, like anybody else."

Could it just be a coincidence? Frederick was probably a fairly common surname ... "What was her first name?" Giselle asked him.

Ruiz's brows furrowed, trying to please her. "Can't remember," he said at last.

Hector's words erupted into Giselle's mind like someone screaming out an old-fashioned telegram. SIEGLIND IS NEAR. TIMETABLE MOVED UP. COME BACK NOW.

Giselle pouted. She'd had plans for this human. "Dammit, Lindy," she muttered.

Ruiz's stoned face lit up. "Lindy! That was her name!"

Lindy was working with the feds? Giselle grinned. Now *that* was information worth having. She pulled out her disposable cell phone and called Hector. He didn't like it when they used phones—he was very aware of the BPI's electronic capabilities—but this was too good to wait. As the phone rang, Ruiz gave her a glazed, inquiring look.

"Change in plans," she told him with a smile.

Chapter 10

At five, an hour before the briefing at the new BPI headquarters, McKenna sent her a text on the new phone: "Everything okay?" Lindy texted back an affirmative and said she would meet them at the briefing. He sent her the address.

The Chicago branch of the FBI was housed in a rather unimaginative brick-shaped glass building on Roosevelt Road, near Douglas Park. The crowded building hadn't the space to squish in a newly created branch of the Bureau, so the BPI was temporarily housed in an empty medical office building in Tri-Taylor, several blocks away. Security was much simpler than Lindy had expected—the front doors just had an intercom system. She pressed the button and was buzzed through immediately, though she paused to look at the door. The intercom system may have been simple, but the doors were steel, and that lock was heavy-duty. She doubted even she could have broken through by force.

Good.

The front door opened into a deserted lobby with four doors. The lettering had been scraped off three of them, so Lindy walked toward the door that said, simply, *Chicago BPI.* She wondered what had happened to the other companies in the building. This much empty, unguarded space made her uncomfortable, and she'd only been there for fifteen seconds.

Through the BPI doors there was a large reception space with people milling around a coffee cart. There were more of them than Lindy had expected—she'd been under the impression that the Chicago BPI was a very small unit—and she paused uncertainly just inside the door.

"Lindy," Alex called. She felt a stab of relief as he shouldered through the crowd with his hand extended as though they hadn't seen each other in days. She understood that this was part of the "convince everyone that Lindy's human" ritual and played along. "Glad you found the place."

"Are all these people part of your team?" she asked, gesturing at the crowd.

"Yes and no." Alex's face was grave. "Our team has access to a group of FBI staff to handle evidence collection and pathology, and they all came over for this initial briefing. With the bodies this morning, everything is a little . . . heightened. Do you want coffee before we start?" As soon as the words were out of his mouth he winced, remembering that she couldn't drink it.

Lindy just smiled and touched his shoulder in a friendly way. "That'd be great."

He led her to the coffee machine, where Lindy put about an inch of dark roast in a paper cup and covered it with a lid. A prop. Then Alex introduced her to the small BPI support staff: an office manager, Sarah Greer; several assistants; a couple of interns. Alex needed to get the briefing started, so he simply pointed out the FBI staff: A liaison agent, Gil Palmer, who was looking bored and impatient to get started; a forensic pathologist and a handful of criminalists; as well as the state medical examiner. The FBI group stood in clusters on the other side of the room from the BPI staff, drinking coffee and looking uneasy, as if they were afraid the BPI team had some sort of communicable disease.

Before Alex could actually call them to attention, Sarah Greer rushed up and asked to speak to him privately. After the agent excused himself to his office, Lindy used the opportunity to collect some gossip, since no one knew about her enhanced hearing. Pretending to sip the coffee, Lindy learned that the FBI group was indeed nervous about being associated with the shade team: There were now three dead teens and a number of dead federal agents, and this mess was starting to look like "a political tar baby," as one sullen criminalist put it.

The FBI group also had a lot of things to say about Alex McKenna, who was apparently the son of the first female director of the FBI. Lindy hadn't known that, and wondered if it explained his ambition and the enthusiasm that bordered on recklessness. Everyone was also talking about the tall, willowy woman standing in a corner with long red hair in a French braid down her back. Alex had briefly introduced her as Jill Hadley, and she was apparently a notorious rising star in the Bureau, the kind of agent who seemed destined to fly up the ranks, maybe even all the way up. Everyone in both the BPI and the Bureau was shocked that she'd crossed over to the BPI team, and speculations about her reasons were flying back and forth. Most of the hypotheses were so ridiculous that Lindy couldn't begin to take them seriously. It sparked her interest in Hadley, though, and she made a mental note to keep an eye on the young agent.

That was all Lindy could gather before Alex finally returned and called the meeting to attention, waving a hand so they would gather around him as he stood in front of one of the office's stark, undecorated walls. Even with the extra Bureau people, there was still a lot more space around their group than was needed. The generic, relatively modern office building had been designed to hold hundreds of workers, rather than a few dozen. Because of the large space, and the crowd of people around her, it took Lindy a moment to realize that Alex was agitated underneath his blank expression. She stepped closer to the front of the group, pretending to take a sniff of her coffee. His pheromones were off, and his pulse was tripping. Something had happened.

"This is where I was planning to make a speech," Alex said without preamble. "But there's been a development, and I'm gonna keep this as brief as possible."

Around her, the agents glanced at one another and passed around minimalist shrugs. No one else knew what was happening—except for Sarah Greer, who looked equally distraught. "I'm Special Agent in Charge Alex McKenna. This"—he motioned to Chase—" is my second in command, Chase Eddy. You've probably met Agents Hadley and Bartell, and our fifth agent, Ruiz, is currently in the Cook County Hospital recovering from the attack that killed my predecessor."

The crowd around Lindy stilled, everyone uncomfortably aware of what had happened to the last group that had pursued the shades. Alex let a moment of silence pass, and then went on. "I'm trying something a little different for our sixth pod member: Instead of another field agent, I have brought in a consultant." He pointed at Lindy, who fought to keep herself from slinking into a shadow. As a rule, shades did not like the spotlight. At-tention made it a lot harder to pick off your prey. "Every-one, this is Lindy Frederick, the last new member of the pod. She's a specialist in language and human behavior, and now we're pulling her out of the private sector and into the pod. She has been studying Ambrose." This was a lie, but no one seemed to suspect it. Lindy listened to the crowd whispering. They were all curious about her, and about Ambrose, who was considered an asset on par with the Ark of the Covenant. But no one was question-ing Alex's story, just as he'd promised.

"She does not have special agent status, but I expect you to give her the same courtesy and respect you would any other team member," Alex went on. "Her methods are a lit-tle different from the Bureau's, but in this case I think that's a good thing." The agents around him grimaced. They were all aware of the Bureau's need for fresh tactics.

Alex paused and looked around the room, meeting the eyes of everyone present. "I know that many of you are dealing with a new city, new home, and new office all at once. On top of all that, we're all coming here with dif-ferent backgrounds, different goals, different strengths. Under normal circumstances we'd have months to get to know one another and figure out how to work together as a unit, but these are not normal circumstances." He turned around, producing a black marker, and wrote the

names of three towns on the bare white wall. Capping
the marker, he faced them again. "Folks, an hour ago our
suspect took four more teenagers captive out of Home-
wood, Lansing, and Heavenly. This is in addition to the
three we believe he still has."

The room erupted into chatter. Lindy felt electric
shock zip through her daylight-dulled brain. Hector had
taken kids *during the day*? That was too bold, even for
him. Shades rarely left their lairs between sunrise and
sunset; they were too weak then. Well, most of them
were. Something must have changed, some kind of cata-
lyst that had caused him to—

Her.

Lindy swore out loud, not caring who heard. Hector
had felt her presence and moved up his plans; that was
the only explanation. All that potential, and he was going
to waste it.

She looked back at Alex, who had lost control of the
room. No, he hadn't—he was simply ignoring it, staring directly at her as the not-so-hushed conversations went on
all around them. They locked eyes for a long moment, and
then Alex gave her a small, weary nod. She found herself
shouting. "Were they related to the previous missing kids?"

The room went instantly quiet, and everyone heard
Alex's low response. "Yes." He turned back to the wall and
began scrawling names under the town names. "Josh Crom-

bie's sister Mimi was taken, along with Chloe Davis's older brother and Danny Cole's half-sister." When he was finished writing, McKenna turned back to meet her gaze, his eyebrows raised. "What are you thinking?"

Every eye in the room turned toward Lindy. She swallowed. *Time to pick a side.* Moving slowly, as if levitating, Lindy threaded through the crowd and went up to McKenna, standing next to him, facing the group. "According to the information from Ambrose, our suspect's name is Hector," she began, her voice shaking just a little, "and I think I know why he's taking siblings." She paused, but none of them were laughing at her or screaming that she was a vampire. Not even whispers. She pushed on. "He's experimenting with transmuting a group of them at once."

Now the crowd rustled uneasily, but Lindy continued, choosing her words to be as efficient and straightforward as possible. "Under the right circumstances, older shades can send orders telepathically to the ones they create. Its a one-way connection." To give them a moment to absorb that, she held out her hand, and without hesitating Alex put the marker into it. She drew a stick figure on the wall, and an arrow leading to a second stick figure below it. "Twins who are transmuted, however, can communicate with both their sire and each other." She drew a second stick figure next to the lower one, and arrows connecting all three. "My theory," she went on, "is that Hector is attempting to find a way to expand that bond, to form telepathic connections among an entire group of shades."

A skeptical voice rang out from the back of the room. "So these kids are what? Lab rats?"

"In a sense," Lindy said soberly. "My research suggests that even shades don't fully understand how the bond between old and new shades works, so trying to repeat a phenomena that's only worked on twins . . . you'd need a lot of different subjects to experiment on."

"In what type of setting?" Chase asked. "Does he need a laboratory? Would it have to be underground? Is there a certain location that might work better than another?"

All very good questions. Lindy tilted her head a moment, considering it. She ignored the whispers that had started from the back of the room, which speculated on everything from how she'd gotten Ambrose to talk to her "fuckability." Some were even drawing a connection between the two. "An actual laboratory wouldn't be necessary," she said finally. "But some lab equipment would be useful: needles and syringes, possibly narcotics to keep the kids sedated. Underground would work, but so would the interior of any building."

The FBI liaison, Palmer, made a noise of frustration. "That could be anywhere. An abandoned warehouse, deserted businesses, sewer systems. Anywhere."

"Why is he being so obvious about it?" asked a new voice. A few people shuffled around, and then she could see Harvey Bartell, the older agent. McKenna had said he'd been on the original team that brought in Ambrose. "I've been hunting shades since Exposure, and I've never heard of one kidnapping and killing people and being so bold about it."

"I don't know," Lindy said. "Shades are predators, hunters with perfect camouflage. There's no reason to . . . I don't know."

"How much time do we have?" came a quiet alto voice from the side. The redhead, Hadley. "How long before this Hector kills the new kids?"

"Hours," Lindy said honestly. She knew Hector as well as she knew herself. The moment he knew she was in town he had grabbed new subjects, the ones that matched the living subjects he had left. "He'll be experimenting with their blood right now, or possibly tonight, when the shades are strongest." And when he'd used up all those kids, he would either come after her or leave Chicago to start over somewhere else.

The agents around her were looking frustrated, helpless. She wished she could say something comforting, but she had no idea how to go about finding Hector's base of operations. She was not an investigator. For the first time, Lindy regretted the transfusions that blurred the connection between her and her brother. This would be so much easier if she could lead the team straight to him.

Alex saw her floundering and stepped forward again. "Here's what we're doing," he announced. "Research and interns, I want you going over the case files from the original group of missing kids, including the three deceased. Recheck everything with the new information in mind, and look for connections to the new victims. Bartell and Hadley, I want you to start files on the kids who just went missing today. Backgrounds, known associates, likes and dislikes, everything you can find. We're low on time, so do what you can over the phone before you start ringing doorbells. Then get together with the others and look for patterns, connections."

He turned to the FBI members, still standing a little apart from the BPI team. "The rest of you, either pitch in with our research or go back to analyzing the evidence from the body dump, plus the autopsies. I'll be coordinating with the labs and the authorities to give you priority on everything." He glanced at his remaining employees. "Lindy, Chase, Sarah, with me, please."

The meeting dissolved into a bustle of individual activity. Alex led them down a short hallway to his office, which was currently just a bare cube with his briefcase tossed over one of the visitor's chairs. Alex sat behind the empty desk, looking first at Sarah Greer. "Sarah, at seven o'clock I'd like you to order pizza and sodas for the staff. Pick someplace decent." He shot a quick, amused glance at Chase. "Someplace with deep dish. It's on me. Come find me and I'll give you my credit card."

The older woman nodded curtly and departed. Chase closed the door behind her.

When the three of them were alone, Alex picked up a pen and toyed with it, his eyes on Lindy. "You did good out there," he said in a low voice. "I could ask you how long you've suspected Hector was experimenting on these kids, but I'm afraid of the answer." Lindy said nothing. "But there's something else you're not telling me."

Lindy gave him a quizzical look, genuinely confused. There were a lot of things she wasn't telling him. "Hector's motive," Alex prompted her. "Why is telepathic communication so important to him? Why is he trying to re-create what he has with you?"

"What he *had* with me," she corrected, a little snappish. "I don't let him into my head anymore. And how am I supposed to know why he wants to talk to his fledglings? What would you do if you and Agent Eddy could speak without words?"

Alex and Chase exchanged a glance, and Lindy could see his answer written plainly on his face. *We* can *speak without words.* "Across great distances," she corrected herself. "In the dark."

Alex's pen went still as he thought over the implications. "From a tactical standpoint," he said slowly, "that would be invaluable. Unlike other forms of communication, we can't listen in on telepathy, or disable it, or steal it. But it still feels like an awful lot of work—with an awful lot of public scrutiny—just for that."

"Is it because he misses you?" Chase asked in a level tone. And Lindy suddenly felt like she'd been punched in the gut.

When she'd finally figured out how to keep Hector out of her mind, it *had* felt unbearably lonely at first. She had spent centuries with a constant connection, a lifeline she could tug whenever she wanted, for big reasons or no reason at all. After she'd detached from him, it felt bleak and hollow for the longest time. But surely he couldn't be killing these children just to fill his head with voices.

Could he?

Before she could come up with an answer, Alex demanded, "And why did you two part ways? What was the ideological dispute?"

Lindy felt herself starting to get angry. "Here's what I can tell you about Hector and his *ideologies*," she said icily. "He believes in an eye for an eye. He believes he's better than you. And he's very angry with humanity. The moment you discovered us, you assumed we were a disease to be cured or eradicated. He thinks you're . . . un-grateful. Rude."

She snapped her mouth shut, suddenly aware that she'd raised her voice. Alex and Chase gave her identical shocked expressions. They probably didn't even realize it, but each of them had moved his hand just a little bit closer to his sidearm. It would have been funny if she weren't annoyed.

"How are we ungrateful?" Chase asked, at the exact same moment that Alex said, "Ungrateful for what?"

She stared at them. "I thought you people had a whole team of scientists working on this," she blurted. "Haven't they told you?" From the men's bewildered expressions, it was clear they had no idea what she was talking about.

Lindy sighed inwardly, suddenly feeling like Sisyphus pushing a rock up a mountain. Doggedly, she forced herself to continue. "The public has been told that we're a parasitic species," she explained. "That we are leeches, bottom feeders, dependent on your blood to survive. But we're not parasitic, we're symbiotic. We help you as much as you help us."

"What the hell does that mean?" Alex asked.

The office door swung open. "I might be able to help with that," said a gruff voice from the doorway. All three of them looked over to see Special Agent Gabriel Ruiz standing in the doorway.

Chapter 11

Alex stared. Just that morning, Ruiz had been gray and frail, as if at any moment his stitches might pop and his intestines come surging out of his middle. Now he was rosy cheeked and bright eyed, standing upright, though his movements were stiff. He was wearing track pants and an oversized T-shirt, looking out of place in the office setting. "Hey, boss," Ruiz said with a tiny smirk. "I feel *better.*"

"What the hell happened to you?" Alex asked.

"Well, it wasn't clean living," Ruiz said cheerfully. "All I know is, I fell asleep after my little excursion this morning, and I woke up looking like this."

"How is that possible?" Chase interjected.

"Giselle." Lindy's voice came out as a whisper, and all three men's heads swiveled toward her. Before any of them could respond she strode over to Ruiz and took his face in her hands, pulling it close as if for a kiss. She examined his eyes and released him with a little grunt. "Yep. His pupils are dilated all to hell. He's been mesmerized."

"And it . . . *healed* him?" Alex asked. Biologists had

135

speculated that shade saliva had some healing properties: It closed up their victims' wounds, allowing them to get away with feeding. But they hadn't confirmed it, and certainly not on this scale.

Lindy nodded. "Shade saliva isn't just a narcotic; it's an immunity boost. Every time one—um, a shade bites a human, it boosts their immunity, their resistance to illness." She added, "And it has the added benefit of healing most wounds."

"Who *are* you?" Ruiz blurted, staring incredulously at Lindy.

"I'm your new friend Lindy," she said with a bright smile.

Alex just looked at Lindy. If there was one area where she would know more than him, this was it. The BPI scientists barely understood mesmerization, since Ambrose wasn't exactly a wiling participant in any experiments.

"How do you know it's not just the painkillers?" Chase asked sensibly.

Lindy cocked an eyebrow at him, then said commandingly, "Ruiz, touch your nose."

The agent obediently lifted a finger to the tip of his nose. Realizing what he'd just done, he scowled and shoved his hands in his pockets, swaying a little as though he were intoxicated. "What the hell, new girl?"

"He's suggestible," Lindy explained, giving Alex a

meaningful look. He understood it to mean *especially to shades.* "Really suggestible, and it's lasted awhile, which tells me someone gave him a *shitload* of shade saliva."

Ruiz gave her a belligerent stare, opening his mouth to demand answers. Alex broke in. "Okay, setting aside the fact that someone got past our security at the hospital, what does this mean? You think it was Giselle?"

Lindy nodded. "I think she's got a hard-on for him, pardon my French." The men all stared at her. Alex didn't think he'd ever heard a woman use that particular expression. Lindy went right over to Ruiz and lifted up the back of his shirt, and Alex realized she was checking for a weapon. He stood there and let her, which indicated just how much the saliva was working on him. "Maybe you want to go back to your desk now?" she offered.

"Yeah," he grunted, backing toward the door. "I guess."

Most of the FBI crew had returned to their headquarters, just down the street, to work on the evidence, leaving only the BPI staff in the building. Alex told Ruiz to help the other members of their pod, and as soon as Ruiz was through the door he wheeled on Lindy. "Why did you check if he was carrying?" he demanded.

She held up her hands. "Easy."

Alex glanced down at himself and realized he'd flipped back his suit coat, exposing his gun. He smoothed it back down again, a little embarrassed. "Sorry. For a second I was picturing . . ." He trailed off, not wanting to say what he was thinking about a fellow agent.

"That he'd start shooting the place up?" Lindy shook her head. "Mesmerized humans can't hold orders in their heads forever—she could tell him to walk in the door shooting, but not to wait three hours and then do it. I don't think he's going to hurt us."

"Okay," he said. "So Giselle healed him. If it wasn't to send him in here with guns blazing, why would she do that?"

"I don't know." Lindy's voice was grim. "She's fixated on him, though. Have you ever seen a cat play with a mouse? It will knock the mouse's legs out, wait until it gets back up and starts to run, then knock its legs out again. She might just be playing with him, or she's planning to use him as a spy—send him in here to poke around and ask questions, and then collect him later."

Alex considered her for a long moment. "Giselle is going to come for him?"

Lindy frowned. "You're not suggesting we use Ruiz as bait?"

"He's a federal agent," Alex said firmly. "He can handle it."

Chase shook his head. "He's basically been roofied, Alex. He's not in his right mind to protect himself from danger. We need to get him someplace safe."

Alex and Lindy exchanged a glance, and Alex knew she was thinking the same thing he was: They had an opportunity here. "Is there a way to sober him up?" Alex asked.

Lindy cocked her head, surprised at the suggestion. "I have no idea. I've never tried to—"

Before she could finish there was a crash from the outer room, and the sound of several people screaming at once.

Chapter 12

When Lindy burst through the doorway, she immediately smelled the blood and had to fight her body's instinctive reaction to it. At least two people were wounded—a BPI assistant and one of the interns—slumped against desks they hadn't managed to step away from, but her enhanced senses suggested they were breathing. There was a third woman lying prone on the floor: the office manager, Sarah Greer. Giselle was crouched on her chest like the incubus in Fuseli's *The Nightmare*. Greer had fainted, but Giselle was holding one of the older woman's hands up to her face, absently sucking on the thumb. Her other hand held a falchion to Greer's throat.

There were a number of guns leveled at Giselle's head, but she ignored them, her bloodred eyes fixed on Lindy, who walked toward her slowly, hands slightly raised.

The last time Lindy had seen her, Giselle was going around in a full-length burka, which she enjoyed because it covered any number of edged weapons. Tonight, however, she wore black leather short-shorts and what appeared to be a black leather corset with a halter top. Platinum and pink hair hung in greasy clumps to her waist. Giselle made no effort to stop the approach, but waited until Lindy was eight feet away before dropping Sarah Greer's limp hand. Blood was still trickling from her thumb.

"Hello, princess," Giselle said happily, her teeth red with blood. The reek of it hit Lindy's nose, and she struggled to retain her composure. She was strong enough to keep the reaction at bay for awhile, but her control was not without limits. "That's far enough," Giselle said, her voice hardening.

"What are you doing?" Lindy hissed. "How did you get in here?"

Giselle absently licked a spot of blood from her lower lip. "Why, Ruiz left the door open for me, didn't you, pet?" Her eyes flicked sideways to Ruiz, who stood mutely at his desk, his face frozen in horror. Lindy cursed herself for not thinking to check the entrance. She had told Alex that Ruiz would have had to complete an order immediately, and then she hadn't even considered that he might have already done it.

Behind Giselle, one of the agents—the older man, Bartell—lifted the muzzle of his weapon. Lindy held up a hand. "Don't shoot her," Lindy barked. Surprised, Bartell and the other agents looked from her to Alex, who had remained by the door to his office. Lindy didn't turn her head to look at his reaction. She knew exactly how well Giselle could throw that blade.

"Why not?" Alex's voice asked from behind her.

"Because it'll just piss her off," Lindy replied absently. She was trying to focus on listening to the empty offices around this room, but it was difficult with so many people and sounds to filter out. "And because there are probably six more shades inside the building right now."

Giselle smirked. "Eight."

"I'm flattered," Lindy said flatly. Alex must have motioned to the other agents, because they all began holstering their sidearms. "What do you want, Giselle?" she asked. "Besides a credit line at Hot Topic."

Giselle blinked, looking innocent. "Why, the same thing we've always wanted, princess. You."

"Me?" Lindy repeated, genuinely surprised. Hector had pursued her in the past, of course, but how could this possibly be about her? Behind her, Alex moved closer until he flanked her right shoulder. Giselle ignored him.

Seeing Lindy's confusion, the shade laughed, a full-throated sound with the edge of insanity. "Of course. This is all about you, princess. It always was. So now I'm walking out of here, and you're coming with me. Or all your pretty new friends will die." Gracefully, she flipped herself off Sarah Greer, coming to her feet. With her blade away from Greer's throat, Bartell stepped forward, raising his gun to Giselle's temple. "We can't let you do that, lady," he growled.

"Really?" Giselle said brightly. "Oh, that's *interesting.* Do you actually think she's one of you?" Whirling around, Giselle twisted around Bartell and pointed his gun at the ceiling before the older agent could so much as squeeze the trigger. Before anyone could respond, the shade lifted the falchion and nicked Bartell's tricep, sending a spurt of bright red blood down his side. Giselle held her hand under the stream for a moment and then shoved Bartell sideways, sending the agent sprawling.

Lindy saw it coming and darted sideways as the other shade flung the handful of liquid at her. It spattered across Alex McKenna's white shirt, and Lindy felt a flash of triumph—she'd kept from "vamping out." But then the other BPI employees gasped, and Lindy realized her error: She'd moved too fast. She froze, not sure what to do.

Giselle laughed again, stalking across the short space between them. Everyone was paralyzed. Giselle raised her bloody hand and rubbed it all over Lindy's face, coating her mouth and nose.

Old as she was, Lindy lost her control and felt the heated snap of blood arousal. The people in front of her gasped again, and she knew the red had blossomed in her eyes. She glanced around, seeing the horror and revulsion on their faces.

Lindy, meanwhile, suddenly felt disgusted with herself. Of course this would happen. It was always going to happen. She should never have agreed to help Alex McKenna in the first place.

Giselle smirked, recognizing the victory. "Come along, then," she sang. "Or I will kill everyone in this room while the others hold you down and make you watch. Even you can't take nine of us."

"Fine." Lindy stepped forward, but she felt Alex's hand on her arm. "Lindy, don't," he urged. "We'll fight for you." Lindy gave him a sad smile. He and Chase, maybe, but Bartell, Hadley, Ruiz, and the remaining assistant looked ready to gift wrap her for Giselle.

She lifted a hand and touched his shoulder, making sure the bracelet on her wrist jingled. Alex's eyes flickered at the noise, but he was enough of a professional not to glance down at the sound. "It's okay, Alex. Take care of your people. And be sure to feed my cat, okay?" She raised her eyebrows, hoping he'd get the message. The agent just nodded, and she couldn't be sure if he'd understood. There was nothing else she could do now, though, so she just stepped away from him and followed Giselle. As they walked out, the other shade blew a kiss toward Ruiz. "See you later, lover," she said merrily, and they were through the door.

An enormous SUV pulled up in front of it, tires screeching to a halt, and Lindy considered her options. She could still run, even hole up somewhere and try to face Giselle and her backup one at a time. Her eyes darted around, taking in the landscape. Maybe—

Lindy felt the prick of the dart. Almost immediately, a sluggish veil descended on her. What the hell? She wheeled on Giselle, who was smirking. Faster than even Giselle could counter, Lindy threw her whole body forward and head butted the shade right in the nose. It made a very satisfying sound as it exploded, but Lindy didn't even get a chance to enjoy it before she passed out. "You bitch," she managed, and then she was out.

Chapter 13

After Lindy and Giselle disappeared through the door-way, Alex caught—not a sound exactly, but more of the sensation of movement all around them. Then the heavy front door—which had a slow-release mechanism at-tached—slammed shut, the square of safety glass shatter-ing and tinkling to the ground. A number of people be-gan to shout at once, but Alex motioned them quiet.

He instructed Ruiz and the assistant, a twenty-five-year-old kid named LaRouse, to start helping the injured and call an ambulance. "Chase, Hadley, with me," he said in a low voice. "The rest of you, stay put until we clear the building." Ruiz looked as if he wanted to protest, but Alex just glared at him.

They moved to the outer edges of the building. Alex posted Hadley at the lobby, so any stragglers couldn't circle back around and evade them. Then he and Chase painstakingly cleared every single empty office. They took no chances, kicking in locked doors and searching every space large enough to hold a human being. Even with no furniture in the building, this took a good fifteen minutes. By the time they got back, the ambulance had come and taken away the injured, leaving him with just Chase, Hadley, LaRouse, and Ruiz, who still looked stricken.

"What now?" Chase asked.

"Now we go after her. Get Noelle on the phone." Chase nodded and headed for a landline.

"Sir?" It was Hadley's voice from behind him. Alex had only had time to exchange a few words with the tall, redheaded woman, but as he turned to face her, the younger agent's eyes were bright and determined. "Why would we rescue a shade from one of her own?" Her tone was heavy with unspoken accusation: *And why did you bring a shade in here?*

"Because she's one of us, too," Alex said shortly. He raised his voice and addressed the room. "Being a shade doesn't make her evil."

"Oh, so she's a *good* monster," Hadley said stubbornly.

Alex glared at her, and then at every remaining member of his team. "Yes, I brought a shade in here. Get over it. There are bigger things in play here than what you think of Lindy."

He marched over to the bulletin board and jabbed a finger at the photos of the missing teenagers. "You heard what that psycho bitch said. Giselle is taking Lindy straight to Hector, who has those kids. And some of them are still alive. We find Lindy, we find the kids." He looked over their heads at Chase, who was hanging up the phone. "Chase?"

"They're still in motion," the other agent reported. "Heading south. Noelle's back in town; she's gonna come straight here."

Alex gave a curt nod. "Call Gil Palmer. Get an FBI breach team together," Alex ordered. "We're going straight to this thing's lair, and we're gonna need manpower."

Chase nodded. "It'll take about twenty, thirty minutes to get them together."

"Fine." Alex looked down, remembering the blood on his shirt. He should have been smart enough to leave a change of clothes here at the office, but for God's sake, they'd only been in Chicago for fifteen hours. Then he remembered Lindy's strange comment about her cat. The hotel was only five minutes away. He told Chase his intention, and asked his friend to get everyone ready to leave in thirty minutes. Then he called for Hadley. "I need a driver," Alex told her.

～

The young woman was silent on the drive to the hotel, her jaw rigid. Alex, who was used to joking around with Chase during quiet moments, started to get uncomfortable. Being someone's boss still felt fairly new to him, and he wondered if he'd come down too hard on the woman for questioning his orders. He scrambled for something to say, some way of breaking the tension and clearing the air between them. He didn't have much time before they reached the hotel.

"So," Alex said finally, "are you a Cubs fan?"

Hadley burst out laughing, which was exactly what he'd been hoping for. "Yes, sir. But I don't have much time to follow them anymore."

"Your file suggests you're a Bureau superstar," he said, just to see how she'd react.

"Yes, sir."

"But you wanted to join the BPI?"

"Yes, sir." She glanced over at him. "It could use a few more superstars, don't you think?"

He couldn't argue with that.

They pulled up to the hotel, and Alex jumped out, running through the lobby at a full sprint. Hadley would follow after securing the car with the valet. Alex ignored the stares of the concierge—they knew there were FBI agents staying there—and headed for his room, where he quickly changed into jeans, a button-down, and a sport coat. Easier to run and fight in, but still a bit formal, in case he came face-to-face with Hector that night. After a moment of hesitation, Alex dug a second room key out of his wallet—Lindy's. He'd had it made when they checked in, just in case.

Her door was kitty-cornered from his. Alex inserted the plastic key and pushed the handle, keeping a foot in the door. He was aware of the cat—he'd had to pay a pet deposit when he checked into the block of rooms—and didn't know if it was the kind of cat that would take off the second a door opened. Or, you know, attack him. Nothing happened, and Alex poked his head into the room. It barely looked occupied—the only signs were a small food and water dish just inside the door, and a packed suitcase set on one of those little stands.

"Do I need to draw my weapon, sir?" came Hadley's voice. Alex jumped and sent a glare over his shoulder. The young agent was standing there with an amused, innocent expression on her face.

"It's possible," Alex said stiffly, "that I'm a little twitchy around cats."

"Yes, sir."

He walked all the way into the room, Hadley on his heels. No sign of the cat, but there was an unopened bag of food propped against the wall on the other side of the suitcase. Alex frowned at it. He'd really felt as if Lindy was trying to tell him something. He eyed the suitcase and waved toward the food bowl. "Would you mind?" he said to Hadley. She stepped forward and began doling out cat food. The moment the kibble hit the bowl, a gray streak flashed toward them from behind the bed. Alex stepped back so it could get by on its way to the dish. Okay, he jumped back. "Well, there's the cat," Hadley observed.

"Yeah." He unzipped the suitcase, exposing clothes, a toiletry bag, a few pairs of shoes—and a brown package, approximately the size of a large picture frame. Alex picked it up, turning it over. The brown paper was sealed tightly, and on the other side Lindy had written in permanent marker: "Lindy's Homemade Cat Treats (Stinky)."

"Is that what you were looking for, sir?"

Alex found a tape-free spot of paper and began ripping. When the box was finally free, he peered cautiously under the lid. And smiled. "You know, I think it is."

~

Lindy woke up angry.

She remembered how waking had often taken her ages as a human, like peeling back many delicate layers in order to go from full REM to full consciousness. There were so many subtle changes to awareness, and they all had to be swum through before she could actually function. As a shade, however, waking up was usually fairly instantaneous, even after whatever it was that had been used to knock her out. One moment, she was fully unconscious. The next, she was alert and spitting mad.

She was also tied down.

The room was nearly pitch-black. While Lindy waited for her shade-enhanced eyes to adjust, she tested her bonds. She was lying on her back in some sort of reclining chair, and she could feel dozens of plastic zip ties fastened around each wrist and forearm, anchoring her to the chair arms. More plastic zip ties anchored her neck to the back of the chair—just loose enough that she could turn her head but not lift it. Some sort of heavy nylon climbing rope secured her legs to the footrest. She wiggled her hands, but the ties were much too tight for her to slide her arms free, even if she drew blood. She would have to pull hard enough to yank off most of the skin on her arms, and although she could probably survive that, her hands would be too damaged to pull the rest of the ties free.

There was also something heavy attached to her left arm, on top of the zip ties. When her eyes finally adjusted Lindy squinted down and saw that a couple of lead vests had been wrapped around her arm. She swore. They'd figured out that the bracelet was a tracker. She supposed she should be grateful that Hector hadn't decided to just cut off her arm to remove it.

Lindy looked around, trying to take in her surroundings. It was a fairly small room, with a counter on either side of her, and a window with closed shades just in front. Some kind of exam room? Everything looked shabby and derelict, as if the decor hadn't been updated since the nineties. She turned her head as far as it would go and tried to peer out of the corner of her eye, but she saw only a door handle, presumably leading to the rest of the building. She sniffed, but the whole room had been masked with vinegar. How obnoxious. She hated having that vulnerable blind spot directly behind her. Hector would have known that, of course. What a wanker.

There was a loud beep and a crackle just behind her, and Lindy jumped, her neck and arms pinching against the zip ties. "Subject is awake, sir," came a low voice from directly behind her. She cursed out loud, in Russian. "Who's there?" Lindy demanded in her best royal tone. "Answer me!"

"My name is Gregor, ma'am." The voice was respectful and professional . . . and maybe a tiny bit familiar? "The king is on his way to see you now."

Lindy suppressed a snort. The king. Of course Hector would want people to call him that. "Have we met before, Gregor? Your voice sounds familiar."

"Yes, ma'am, in New York in 1983. I was with Hector's security force."

Lindy winced, glad he wouldn't see it. "Ah."

The door handle turned, and then a light switch

flicked on, sending bright fluorescents bursting into her sensitive vision. Lindy blinked hard, seeing spots. Her brother really was a dick. "Hello, Hector," she said with a sigh. She didn't bother turning her head.

"Hello, Sieglind."

Her brother stepped into view. He had been a tall man back in their day, though now his height was considered average. He had her dark blond hair, though his was fashionably cropped in the latest style, and sharply slanted cheekbones directing the eye to his square chin. His bright blue eyes were almost always dancing, a genetic quirk that had gotten them out of many scrapes when they were children running around the castle. He wore a stylish suit with no tie, open at the collar, and looked in every way like a Good Guy, the kind of person who would let his dates win at pool and charm the pants off their parents. But he was a killer, and Lindy was the one person who never forgot that.

He gazed at her, waiting for a response, but she just watched him silently. He didn't like that. Lifting an arm, he snapped his fingers at someone behind her. She *hated* not being able to see. "You can begin now," Hector commanded. "The drug has worn off."

The person stepped into view: a black woman, in her midthirties maybe, slender and nervous looking. She was carrying a tray filled with medical supplies: tubes, syringes, empty vials, even Band-Aids. Lindy heard the woman's pulse jumping around in her chest and realized she was human. That wasn't like Hector at all. She cocked an eyebrow at her brother.

"Oh, this is Stella," he said dismissively. "She's a hematologist. Helping me with my studies."

Stella began pulling on surgical gloves. Lindy couldn't resist asking her brother, "What did you shoot me with?" She didn't know of any drug that could affect a shade's system. Then again, she didn't exactly experiment.

Hector smiled broadly, enjoying the moment to brag. "Methamphetamine. It's man-made, so our bodies don't quite know how to process it. As it turns out, they shut down for a time."

Lindy absorbed this knowledge as Stella pulled on surgical gloves, tied rubber tubing around Lindy's right arm, and insert a needle to draw blood. As she worked, her eyes lowered, Lindy saw dark bruises on the woman's upper arms and one wrist. They were clearly finger marks, as if she'd been grabbed and maneuvered around like furniture. Her face was expressionless, but her hands were trembling.

"It's all right," Lindy said quietly. Stella looked up, meeting her eyes for the first time. She looked surprised. "I'll be still," Lindy told her.

Stella nodded tightly and continued her work, but

her shoulders had relaxed a little bit. While the vials of blood began to fill, Hector paced a little, peering through the blinds, checking his watch. He wasn't used to being ignored, but he also didn't want to speak first and reveal his annoyance. Lindy suppressed a smile. Some things didn't change.

The young woman filled eight vials with her blood, enough that Lindy started to feel the loss. Her body would replenish it quickly, but she was going to need to feed before the end of the night, especially if there was fighting. And God, Lindy hoped there would be fighting.

When the last vial was filled, Stella set it on the tray next to the others and peeled off her gloves, looking to Hector for orders. "Leave us," he said flatly. "Begin the testing."

The young woman nodded and left the room with the tray. Lindy heard, rather than saw, Gregor follow her out. Hector leaned against the counter, watching her expectantly.

"So, Sieglind," he said finally. "You don't call, you don't write."

"I get that way about people who try to kill me."

"In New York?" He scoffed. "Please. That was barely a real attempt."

She felt anger rising and tamped it down again. "And yet Rhys died."

"Who?"

She recognized the bait for what it was and stayed silent. After a moment, Hector sighed and inclined his head. "Okay, fine. I'm sorry your little boyfriend died. I never thought he would have made the cut, but whatever. That's all in the past. We need to think about the future." He frowned. "I need to know how you shut me out."

Lindy said nothing for a long moment, but this time Hector was prepared to wait her out. He straightened up so he could tower over her, arms folded.

"Why did you waste those children?" Lindy asked instead.

He waved a hand. "The experiment failed. That happens with lab animals. It's not like they were the first." He saw the surprise on her face and chuckled. "Oh, come on, Sieglind. You didn't really think I just started these trials? I've been working on this for years. This crop is only the first time I've allowed anyone to notice."

"Because of me," she said flatly. "To draw me out, force me to move against you?"

He shrugged. "My experts have suggested that studying your blood will help them figure out how to repeat the effect. I had to get your attention somehow. And it worked, didn't it? You got careless. You became obsessed." He shook his head fondly. "I have to admit, though, you gave me a run for my money. Do you know how many hackers I had to eat before I found one that could track your activity on the Darknet? I mean, talk about waste."

Lindy made an effort not to clench her jaw. "All this just to boost the telepathy?"

"Of course. In part, anyway." He looked a little confused. "I thought you of all people would get it, Lindy. That's the dream, isn't it? One smooth, unblemished conversation between like minds? Its what you and I used to have, and its what all of them want. To never have to be alone, ever again. The humans have all these little devices for constant communication, but their devices have been tainted. They can be hacked, corrupted, broken. I'm going to beat them at their own game. Shades will be even more superior than we are now, and they'll see our advantages and tremble."

She let out a short laugh. He was just so earnest, so ridiculous. He really saw himself as the messiah of vampires. King, indeed. "You don't believe me?" he demanded.

"I believe *you* believe it," she countered. "But you're lying to yourself again, Hector. You might want to show off for mankind, but you're not going to stop there. You're still angry about New York. You'll use your little telepathic commando force to kill people."

He smoothed down his perfect lapels. "You're being

too emotional, Sieglind. Look at the numbers. Too many of us died during Eradication, and now those who remain have to go underground. And humanity is suffering for it. Surely you've noticed the rise in illnesses. Everything is worse, from autism to allergies. There simply aren't enough of us to keep humanity's diseases from spreading."

"So make more," she broke in. "You love making fledglings; why not just focus on that?"

"*Because,*" he said with exaggerated patience, as if she were a belligerent child, "while our numbers have decreased, theirs have skyrocketed. The planet is overpopulated; it's dying. These humans don't care: they'll be dead before it truly expires. But we'll still be here. The only way to save us, to save *all* of us, is to cull the herd."

Lindy shook her head in disgust. He was like one of those evangelical preachers who picked and chose certain bits of the Bible in order to justify any atrocious behavior they felt like committing. "You make it sound so noble, but we both know you want revenge," she said in a low voice. "Plain and simple. You're pissed about Eradication, and you want them to know it. Now that we've been exposed, you've got your chance to—" She stopped short as the realization hit her. Hector raised his eyebrows inquiringly. "You *sent* Ambrose to get caught," she said accusingly. "I can't believe I didn't see it before. Does he know he's the sacrificial lamb?"

One side of Hector's mouth turned up in the devilish smile she knew so well. "Of course not. To be fair, I never thought the American courts would let it go on this long. I thought for sure they'd have killed and dissected him by now." He shrugged.

The fury rose in her until it seemed to fill her up, like a balloon under her skin. Hector had exposed thousands of years of secrecy, out of a petty grudge? "You call yourself a king," she spat, "but do you know how confused and terrified our people are over this? How *lost*? All so you could play your petty games? You son of a bitch."

"Careful," he hissed, real anger naked on his face. "That's *your* mother, too." Catching himself, Hector paced a few steps toward the window, preening. "Anyway. You don't get to talk to me about responsibility and leadership. You walked away, remember? And now Giselle tells me you've joined up with those cretins, hunting down our own kind." He shook his head in disgust. "You whore. I never thought you'd actually *work* for them."

She blinked, surprised. "You must have known the BPI tracked me down. You were the one who sent them." She still didn't understand why he'd given the BPI her name just as he was sending his own people after her. It probably didn't matter at this point, but the longer he talked, the more time Alex McKenna had to find her.

Hector's eyes narrowed. "I absolutely did not. I knew they caught up with you in Cincinnati because my people were also there. I assumed you'd kill or mesmerize them."

"You *just* said you got a hacker to find my current ID, tracing my Darknet activity," she shot back. "Ambrose gave the same ID to the feds. Are you trying to tell me that your pet worm has gone rogue?"

Hector tilted his head, his irritated expression falling away as he thought that over. "That's very interesting," he mused, in that arrogant way he had, where he forgot anyone else was in the room. "I've been briefing Ambrose on our efforts, but I wonder what our Agent McKenna did to convince him to share." He waved a hand dismissively. "It doesn't matter now. The point is, I never thought you'd actually become their pet. You act as if I betrayed you, but you betrayed our entire kind."

She opened her mouth to remind him that he'd *tried to kill her,* but stopped herself. They were just going to go around and around again. This was getting her nowhere. "So what now, Hector? You've got me here; you've taken my blood. Is this the part where you try to convince me to join your cause? Or are you gonna do both of us a favor and just kill me?"

Hector scowled at her. "I can't kill you; I may need more of your blood," he retorted. He gestured at the small room. "Get comfortable." He turned on his heel and strode toward the door, but paused just behind Lindy, where she couldn't see what he was doing. "By the way, Giselle has requested some . . . recreational time with you. I saw no reason to deny her." He smirked. "You girls have fun."

The door slammed behind him.

Chapter 14

At two in the morning, Ruiz was still at the office, seated at an empty desk out of the way of the main traffic. After the ambulances left, the SAC had actually tried to send Ruiz home, or back to the hospital with Bartell and Greer and the others, but Ruiz managed to convince him that the shade saliva had mostly worn off by now. He begged McKenna to let him stay and be in on the bust. He'd actually threatened to get down on his knees for the begging, which had either frightened or amused McKenna enough to let him stick around—as long as he didn't touch any evidence or have access to a weapon. Ruiz had been happy to play by those rules if he got another run at Giselle.

And, if he was being honest with himself, he was also a little afraid to go home.

Instead, he sat and flipped through his own old files on the missing kids, keeping an eye on the rest of the team as they tried to figure out where the hell to find this Hector guy. After Giselle's big shade offensive—another first in the history of the Bureau—Alex McKenna had announced that Lindy's status as a shade was to remain absolutely confidential to this team, or they would all find themselves on the lookout for vampires in Antarctica at best, or jailed for treason at worst. Ordinarily Ruiz would have laughed off this kind of threat, or gotten angry, or maybe disobeyed just to spite the bastard, but he was just too confused—and too humiliated by his own treachery—to protest.

So they'd all stayed quiet, even when Palmer and a couple of backup agents returned to the BPI bullpen, looking incredulous. No one could believe that this mysterious species, which had been so elusive in the months since their discovery, had actually invaded the office of the Chicago BPI en masse and taken away their new consultant. It seemed far-fetched even to Ruiz, and he'd lived through it.

He finished rereading the Crombie file and set it aside. On the other side of the bullpen, McKenna and Eddy were talking to a woman he didn't know, a hot Asian chick who was tall and skinny enough to play for the WNBA. Apparently Lindy Frederick had been wearing a high-tech tracking bracelet, and this newcomer, Liang, was responsible for monitoring it. Ruiz had been close enough to hear her explain that the signal had disappeared at an intersection in downtown Heavenly, after a short pause in the same place. She had hypothesized that someone had discovered the bracelet's tracking capabilities and waited long enough to meet a second group, which had some way of removing the jewelry or blocking the signal.

McKenna was looking more and more frustrated as each minute ticked by and the chances increased that Hector would cut his losses and run. He had to know the BPI would be hunting him and his pet psycho bitch, and when he finished whatever he was doing with Lindy, the smart move would be to bail. At that point, he'd either kill the kids or transmute them, and this whole operation would have failed. Creadin would have died for nothing. Ruiz couldn't have that.

Well, you're not doing any good reviewing your own notes, he told himself. He looked around. They had all improvised desk space in the main room for the moment, and Hadley's was directly behind him. Ruiz wheeled his chair backward until he was in her peripheral vision. She was bent over photos of the body dump, which the FBI team had printed off in full color at their fancy office. "How's it going?" he asked her. She just grunted, not bothering to look up. "Are those just the crime-scene shots, or is the pre-autopsy stuff there, too?" he tried. Before an autopsy actually began, the ME spent a few minutes photographing the body and collecting any evidence that may have clung to the skin.

Reluctantly, Hadley tore her eyes away from the file. "Aren't you supposed to be lying low?"

He raised his eyebrows. She was what, twenty-five? Pretty ballsy, but Ruiz liked strong women. He looked down at the files. She'd already flipped through three-quarters of the photos. "Let's trade," he suggested. "I'll look at those, you look through my files on the missing kids. Maybe you'll catch something I missed."

Hadley kept her poker face in place, but he could see the wheels turning behind her eyes. She wanted to be the one to break this case open, and finding a mistake in the old files would be a hell of a way to do it. It was irresistible. "Okay, fine," she said. They swapped files.

Ruiz eagerly turned the photo pages over, skipping straight to the pre-autopsy shots. He'd seen the body dump in person.

At first, he didn't notice anything they hadn't seen at the culvert. The bodies had been treated drastically different. Budchen still looked mostly unharmed, although the ME had immediately spotted some needle marks on the smooth underside of her arm that hadn't been visible the way they were lying. There were a number of close-up images of the marks, but that didn't tell Ruiz anything. Just out of curiosity, he flipped to the photos of Harrison to see if the kid had the same needle marks. He did. Ruiz put the pictures side by side, frowning at them. Something felt off. He flipped through the rest of the Budchen photos and found a good one of the tops of her wrists.

Ligature marks.

Back to Harrison's photos, and yes, there were ligature marks on the tops of his wrists, too. Ruiz—and presumably, the other agents—had been so busy seeing the differences between the two bodies that they'd missed this similarity: the outsides of the wrists were damaged by some kind of restraints, but the undersides were unmarred.

He picked up the phone at his desk and dialed Jessica Reyes, the pathologist who was conducting the autopsies. Her caller ID must have said BPI offices, because she sounded very annoyed when she answered. "I *told* you, I will have the reports as soon as humanly possible," she snapped, by way of greeting. "Calling me every ten minutes is only making this process slower, and—"

"Jess, it's Gabriel Ruiz," he interrupted. "Sorry to bother you while you're cutting."

"Oh," she said, sounding surprised. "Hey, Gabriel. I'm just finishing the second autopsy. What do you need?"

"I was looking at the photos, and saw that only one side of the wrists has a ligature mark."

"Yes, I noticed that, too."

"What does it mean? They were tied to a chair?"

"No," she said without hesitation. "Even with a hard-backed chair, we usually see some abrasions on the underside of the wrist. The victims struggle and flail, and they end up with at least the top layer of skin rubbed away. Here, the skin is perfect."

"Anything else weird coming up in the autopsy?" There was a long pause, and he could feel her reluctance. Like many medical examiners, Jessica Reyes did not like jumping to conclusions, or making guesses. In a case like this, where a BPI asset was at risk, it would only make her more cautious, not less. She didn't want to send anyone off on a wild goose chase when the bad guys had their asset. "Come on, Jess," he wheedled. "We go back. This is just between us."

Another, briefer pause, and then she said, "Well, you'll have the report in an hour anyway, so I doubt it matters. There's some indication that the victims were both sort of half lying, half sitting when they died."

"How can you tell?"

"The lividity. The shades didn't leave a lot of blood in either body, but what there was had pooled downward into the buttocks, lower back, and ankles, rather than evenly across the body."

Ruiz tried to picture it. "Like they were sitting in a La-Z-Boy?"

"I don't think they make armchairs that you could tie restraints to, not without a whole lot of trouble," she reported. "But I suspect the chair *was* padded, given the lack of abrasions."

A padded chair that reclined, but not an armchair. What other chairs came with padding? Office chairs didn't recline that much, and neither did waiting room chairs.

Then it hit him. "Thanks, Jess," he said hurriedly. "You saved the day."

"What did I—" But he'd already hung up.

"You found something."

Ruiz jumped. Hadley was standing right behind him, looking over his shoulder. She'd made about as much noise as a cat. He eyed her. "You any good with computer databases?"

"Yes," she said, her voice matter of fact.

"Then you're probably better than me. Pull up a chair, we're about to crack this."

Chapter 15

"A dentist's chair?" Alex repeated, giving Ruiz an appraising look. They were in his office, with Chase at his elbow. "Even dental clinics must have some kind of security. And where are they taking the kids during the day?"

Ruiz gestured to Hadley, who stepped forward and laid several Google Earth printouts in front of him. "Sir, we found an abandoned private dental clinic just outside of Heavenly. Closed two years ago due to a malpractice suit. This is where we think they are."

Alex looked from one to the other, impressed. "Let me make a call," he said finally.

Deputy Director Harding pulled strings to get them immediate access to one of the Bureau's satellite feeds. Ten minutes after *that*, Bureau technicians had confirmed the presence of nine warm bodies—the surviving teenagers, most likely, and a human they didn't know about—and more movement just outside: the shades, loading things into enormous moving vans. Their body temperatures weren't high enough to register on thermal, but Lindy's hunch had been correct: they were packing up.

When Alex hung up the phone, he ordered Palmer to get their team mobilized. Then he turned to Chase. His friend wrinkled his nose in annoyance. "Shit, Alex, you know I hate that look."

"Protocol would have me send you, while I stay here," Alex began. "We're reversing it. You're in charge here. I'm going with the extraction team."

Chase shook his head. "No way, man. You can't play cowboy anymore. You wanted to be the SAC, and you're good at it. I'm going."

"No, you're not." Alex gestured around the office. "I'm good at action, Chase. Making things move. But there's a solid chance that this isn't going to work, and then this team is going to need a strategist. That's you."

"Bullshit. This is your plan, and you think responsibility means going down with the ship. It's a romantic idea, but this is the twenty-first-century FBI, Alex. We have a chain of command for a reason."

Alex's face hardened. "Do I need to remind you that we're not exactly playing by Bureau rules these days? The BPI is new, and it does things differently. That fluidity exists for a reason."

Chase opened his mouth to protest again, but Alex overrode him. "This isn't a debate, Agent Eddy. You're in charge here; I'm going with the team."

Chase glared. "You're pulling rank on me?"

Alex tasted sourness, but he had already committed. "Yeah. That's an order."

"Fine," Chase snapped. "Have it your way. But by God, Alex, you better not be doing this to us over a goddamned girl."

He stalked out of the office.

～

Alex's team nearly broke the sound barrier on the way south, arriving in less than twenty minutes, at three thirty in the morning. One SUV did a quick drive-by: The shades had stopped loading, but the moving van was still sitting there. The building appeared to be completely dark from the road, but when they parked a block ahead and snuck back, Alex could make out snatches of light filtering through the blinds. They were in the right place.

The building had three entrances: a front door, a back door, and a large side door that had been used for large deliveries when the dental office was operational. This was where the shades' truck was parked. "How do you want to do this, boss?" asked Hadley, who sat in the passenger seat next to Alex. There were two more agents behind them, and fourteen total in the trailing SUVs. Everyone was waiting on Alex's order before they went in.

Alex considered it. He was still feeling a little out of sorts after the argument with Chase, but he told himself it was time to get his head in the game, or he'd have more than hurt feelings to worry about. The research team had dug up the building's blueprints, but they still didn't know where any of the shades were within the building. If they went in right now, with no other intelligence, there was nothing to stop Hector and his people from killing the teenagers on the spot.

There was also the problem of weapons. They'd brought guns, Tasers, and even a few KA-BAR knives, which weren't exactly protocol. The problem was that almost none of it had been tested against shades before. They still knew so little about their physiology.

It made Alex wary of just storming all the entrances. He remembered the package in the backseat, still in the box labeled "Cat Treats." He thought of the way Giselle had called Lindy "princess," and how Lindy had never once demonstrated the least bit of physical fear. If she was who he thought she was . . . maybe they didn't need to storm the place.

He grabbed the walkie-talkie and the building plans. "We're gonna flush them out. I want three people on each exit, waiting outside to stop the shades as they come running out. Remember: They're faster than us, so keep them as far from your person as you can. Taser on sight, then arrest them if they go willingly: secure with plastic zip ties and hoods." Gil Palmer relayed the command to his agents, dividing out the door assignments. When the line went silent again, Alex added, "The rest of you are with me. We're going in the side entrance, with two priorities: secure the kids and free Lindy. I have a feeling if we can get her loose, she'll do a lot of our work for us."

"Yes, sir." Beside him, Hadley raised an eyebrow. "Any final advice on how to hurt them, sir?"

"We know they need blood, so try to force them to lose as much as possible, as fast as possible," Alex told her. "And if you can detach the head from the body, I'm pretty sure it's game over."

Hadley nodded, her expression unreadable. When this was over, Alex thought, he was really going to need to get to know his team better. "Everyone geared up?" he said into the walkie-talkie. The people in his vehicle nodded, holding up their helmets. The night was warm, but every man and woman under his command wore turtlenecks, gloves, and long plexiglass visors that went down past their chins. He'd learned his lesson about shade saliva with Ruiz. "Let's go."

~

It was somewhat pathetic, Lindy thought, that after all

her years of life, all the wars and tragedies and accidents she'd seen, her own downfall would come at the hands of a few strips of plastic.

Wiggle and pull as she might, she couldn't get even a single limb free of the fucking zip ties. Out of desperation, she even tried to slide her arm out by letting her skin tear off, hoping it would have time to heal before anyone realized what she'd done, but the moment she began, the scent of her blood brought two of Hector's minions running. They'd tightened all the remaining straps and even added on a few more.

After awhile, even Lindy had to admit that she was just fucking stuck.

She settled back to wait, listening hard to glean information. From elsewhere in the building, she could hear several people crying—probably the teenagers. There was an occasional scream, and some begging: "Please, I want my mom, please . . ."

Hearing this, Lindy's eyes burned with angry tears. She knew that this was all part of Hector's plan: he could have easily mesmerized the kids to stay calm and quiet, but he wanted to let Lindy stew, let her listen, let her get upset. It would make her off balance, emotional—and Hector *loved* when she got emotional. Classic male mentality, and classic Hector. It was actually sort of comforting to realize his patterns of behavior hadn't changed in fifteen hundred years.

Thinking about patterns of behavior actually gave Lindy an idea, though. She renewed her escape efforts, but stopped focusing on getting past the zip ties and turned her attention to the chair itself. Underneath the padding, the construction was solid: made of some kind of heavy metal that didn't even rattle when she shook her left arm or her legs. The right arm of the chair, however, had a little give to it. Lindy smiled.

Slowly, as quietly as possible, she applied pressure, first in one direction, then another. She didn't feel a change at first, but then little by little, the bolts began to deform and loosen. Lindy could feel the metal flexing under the pressure, but there was no way to know how much farther it had to go before the arm of the chair would rip all the way off. Then she could—

With no warning, the door behind her slammed open again, and Lindy went still as Giselle sauntered into the room, a smug pout on her bloodred lips. Literally, there was blood on her mouth; she had just finished feeding, probably from one of the teenagers. She had changed into a black leather sheath dress that barely covered her ass, and her favorite weapon, the falchion, was strapped to one thigh. Her stringy pink and white hair was pulled back into a bun so messy it may as well have not existed. There was no sign of her facial injury. Lindy felt a little disappointed about that.

"Hey, Giselle, how's your nose?" Lindy asked cheerfully.

The other woman's smile was cruel. "It's fantastic, thanks so much for asking." She painstakingly wiped her lips with the tip of one finger. "Healing was a bitch, of course, but Hector let me have one of the children who wasn't useful anymore. Just to be sure, I drank him all down."

She tried to hide her fury, but Giselle saw it anyway and gave her a victorious smile. Lindy reminded herself that just as Giselle knew her pressure points, she knew Giselle's. "So how *are* things going with you and my brother?" she asked, painting a bright smile on her face. Instantly, Giselle's expression clouded over.

"It's fantastic. Better than it's ever been," she said coolly. Then she climbed onto Lindy's lap, straddling the much older shade and leaning forward so her ample breasts were in Lindy's face. "Of course, there's always room for improvement. Or for extra participants."

Ew. "Grow up, Giselle."

Giselle just gave her a wicked smile. "Oh, I did grow up, Sieglind. I've learned so much since Eradication." She hopped off Lindy's lap and drew the falchion, the metal singing as it came free. "Don't worry; I'm going to show you." Hitching her hip on the left side of Lindy's chair,

Giselle let the tip of the blade rest at the hollow of Lindy's throat, savoring the moment. For Giselle, it had been a long time coming.

There was a crash from just outside the room, and men's voices began shouting. Giselle's triumphant smile flickered. She glanced toward the door, and Lindy saw the best chance she was going to get. With every bit of power available to her, Lindy wrenched her right forearm, making no attempt to be quiet or subtle. The metal caught, and then with a scream the entire arm of the reclining chair broke off.

Giselle tried to react, and up against a younger or less experienced shade her reflexes would have been enough to dodge. But Lindy was the second-oldest vampire on the planet, and she clubbed Giselle across the side of the head with the metal chunk hard enough to throw Giselle backward, dropping the blade.

Right in Lindy's lap.

She grabbed the falchion, slicing her fingers a little, and managed to twist it in her wrist so she could force it across the zip ties on her left arm. The blade made a long, shallow cut as it went, but Lindy paid no attention. Giselle staggered up from the floor, leaning against the wall for balance.

"You *bitch*," Giselle screamed, but Lindy ignored her. She was carefully cutting the looser zip ties holding her neck to the back of the chair. Giselle darted toward her, but Lindy reversed the falchion in her hand and managed to stab Giselle in the shoulder before the other shade lurched back again. Giselle let out a bellow of frustration, turned, and leapt through the window behind her.

~

The side door of the clinic led to a tiny hallway that opened straight into a large, relatively open room in the middle, where there had once been hygienists' desks and file cabinets. This large space was surrounded by smaller chambers and hallways that the patients would have used for examinations. Alex had guessed that the shades were keeping the kids in the patient rooms and using the open space, which had the added benefit of no windows, for a makeshift lab. He'd been right about that, but by the time he and the six agents behind him entered the room, the shades had all heard and sensed them coming, and done the logical thing, from a tactical point of view: they'd cut the lights.

Alex skidded to a halt inside the tiny hallway, holding up a fist for the team to stop with him. Behind him, there was a little light from the street lamps. In front of him, the darkness was absolute. Alex was pretty sure if he'd taken two more steps into the room, the shades would have picked him off.

"Bureau of Preternatural Investigations," he bellowed into the darkness. "You're under arrest!"

No one flipped on the lights, but about eight feet to either side of him Alex heard low, insidious chuckles. That was enough for him. "Hadley, sticks," he ordered, and behind him, Agent Hadley reached into a pocket and pulled out a handful of industrial-size glow sticks, breaking the wad of them with both fists. Alex sensed movement to his right as one of the shades darted forward to stop her. He reflexively fired a low burst that caused a high-pitched scream. Hadley threw the sticks, sending just enough light into the room for them to make out the figures advancing on them.

Alex started shooting, stepping forward into the room so the other agents could fan out a little and get clear shots. The noise from the weapons was deafening, but all around him, Alex could still hear muffled young voices crying for help with renewed vigor. They were in the patient rooms, just as he'd anticipated. Unfortunately, between their cries and the gunfire, he could no longer hear the shades.

One of them popped up just in front of him, and Alex and the agent at his shoulder—Simonson was his name—fired. The muzzle flash illuminated two other shades behind that one, and for a moment it was a shooting gallery. The shades seemed to race toward them in stop-motion speed, or like those old zoetropes. They were so fast, and the bullets flew so thickly, that Alex prayed the doors trapping the teenagers were strong. Then a shade leapt at him from above—*Christ, they could jump*—and Alex couldn't get his sidearm up in time. The shade hit him with its full weight, slamming him into the floor.

He landed on his back with the shade scrabbling at his helmet, trying to get to his neck. Alex tried to bring up the gun but the shade—a male, bigger than him—slapped it out of his hand, where it went skittering into the darkness. Pinning him, the shade ripped off Alex's visor and lowered his head—and then he was suddenly, simply, gone. Alex blinked and sat up. Just behind him, his team was crowded together, blocking the exit and trying to pick off shades. Hadley crouched and reached out a hand to help Alex up.

"Where did he go?" Alex shouted.

"Who?"

Just then, the room flooded with light.

Chapter 16

After Giselle's abrupt exit through the window, it had taken Lindy a few minutes to get herself fully loose. During that time she heard a lot of screaming and gunshots. Alex's voice was definitely in the mix, and her spirits lifted a little.

Conscious of the danger, she slipped to the door and peeked through a crack, trying to get some idea of the layout and the situation. It was fairly dark in the big space outside the door, but she had no trouble making out Alex McKenna at the front of a cluster of agents in visors as they shot at the shades hidden all around the room. There was no sign of her brother, which worried her.

Hector's people were slinking along the floor, through the shadows, while the BPI agents were distracted by one or two of them making noise. A few of the shades were attempting to sneak away to the exits, but most of them—seven, by her count—were creeping along the walls, intent on getting close to Alex's group and cutting them off. Cutting them down.

Alex stumbled forward a little to give his team more

room. A large shade—Gregor—saw his opportunity and dove at the BPI agent. Shit. Lindy raced forward and hit him hard, her momentum shoving Gregor all the way off Alex and into the cheap plaster wall. Lights, they needed lights, or Alex's team would be useless. Spotting a switch next to one of the office doorways, Lindy picked her way around the bullets and flicked it on, wincing at the transition.

Now able to see the room, the federal agents adjusted quickly and began shooting at the shades—but they were too fast, and they could survive plenty of wounds before they'd bleed out. They were gaining ground. "Alex!" Lindy shouted. The lead agent looked up. "You have something for me?"

He gave her a short nod and grabbed at the back of his pants, pulling two small objects from where they'd been tucked into his belt. Lindy grinned as the twin push daggers came sailing through the air, slow enough for her to pluck them out by the handles. She dropped Giselle's falchion on the ground in favor of her preferred weapons.

The push daggers looked like tiny swords, with four-inch blades—just long enough to sever a man's spinal cord—that attached to solid oak handles shaped like *T*s. Lindy grasped each handle so that the blade protruded between her middle and ring fingers on each hand, and instantly each weapon became an extension of her. In the middle of the firefight she embarked on her own stealth mission, spinning around the room to attack shade after shade. With each one she swept the blades across a number of major arteries: brachial, aortic, femoral, whatever she could get close to. The shades dropped to the ground, bleeding out too fast to heal.

She managed to take out three shades by herself before they realized she was among them. By then, however, they'd snatched two of the agents out of the hallway and were drinking them dry. The other agents had begun to break formation, inching forward in hopes of rescuing their teammates before they died of blood loss. Lindy cursed and started running forward to help, but Alex waved her on. "Get the kids!" he shouted. Lindy understood: She was the only one far enough in the room to make it to the other patient chambers.

Before she could respond, however, she saw light glint off a blade raised high in the air. Giselle. "Behind you!" she screamed at Alex. He immediately spun to the side, and Giselle's blade sliced the air where his head had been. She'd left the building, recovered a backup blade from somewhere, and come up behind the agents . . . which meant whoever had been left to guard the door was probably dead. Giselle started to rush Alex, but the agent had his gun up and was firing rounds into her heart. "The kids!" he yelled over his shoulder.

Lindy bolted at the first patient room she saw, the one next door to her former cell. Inside, she found another ancient dentist chair with a heavyset kid of eighteen or nineteen strapped to it—only he just had one zip tie per limb. He was wearing jeans and a rumpled T-shirt, and he smelled terribly of body odor and fear. His forearm was exposed, and she could see multiple puncture marks dotting the white skin. His eyes were open, but dull.

"Hi. What's your name?" She sliced through the zip ties as she spoke. The kid's glazed eyes rolled over to her.

"Josh," he said hoarsely.

"Do you think you can walk, Josh?"

"No."

"Too bad. You have to." In a much-practiced movement, she tucked one of the daggers into the back of her pants and reached down to drag the kid up. "My sister," he mumbled. "I swear I heard my sister screaming."

"I'll get her, too." Lindy looked around the room and decided the kid's best chance was the window, but this one was boarded up. She leaned back on one heel and kicked a foot—straight through the plywood. Oops.

The kid's eyes went wide. "You're a vampire," he blurted.

"Yes, but I'm with the good guys." She kicked the rest of the wood in, creating a hole big enough for Josh to climb through. "Come on." She tilted her head at the window, but he just looked at her with wide, terrified eyes. Lindy sighed, pushing back a strand of hair that had come loose from her ponytail. "Josh. You wanna stay here, or you wanna go sit in a nice armored FBI car?"

He went through the window.

~

After six or seven shots to the heart, Giselle had roared with anger, ignoring the already healing holes in her chest from Alex's gun, and charged forward—not toward Alex, but past him into the main part of the room, toward the other shades. He began laying down cover for Hadley, who was trying to get to one of the injured agents, but he heard a screech of surprise and rage as Giselle nearly ran into Lindy, who had returned from the first patient room. The two women both went still for a moment, snarling at each other in a way that was more animal than human, and Alex wondered how he had ever been surprised to learn Lindy was a shade. Then their blades connected with a singing crash of metal.

For a moment, Alex—and pretty much everyone else in the room—just stared at them, trying to follow the shade-speed fight with his human eyes. Both women had obviously spent a lot of time with those blades; they wielded them the way Alex wielded his thumb. They fought with no discernible martial arts style, but a blend of anything and everything that was well suited to knife fighting. Giselle threw Lindy over her shoulder in a move that looked like modern aikido, but Lindy regained her feet in a sweeping balanced move that reminded him of capoeira. There was no style, but there was every style, and Alex realized with a shock that these women might have predated some forms of martial arts.

"Boss!" Hadley screamed. Alex tore his eyes off Lindy and Giselle and ran over to help Hadley pull a wounded agent from the shade who was trying to tug him away. When the agent was safely behind the choke point, Alex glanced around, taking stock of the rest of the battle.

And it was a *battle*.

Lindy had taken out three shades during her terrifying lethal ballet, and Alex's team had shot down two others, who had both taken so much lead that they'd sunk to the floor. One of them had grabbed a female agent, Raver, and drunk a good deal of her blood, but Hadley had shot it so many times in the head that it eventually fell still. Raver was alive, but so pale that he didn't think she'd last long. Another agent had died in the same manner, and two more behind him had been killed by Giselle's weird machete thing. The BPI team was slowly gaining ground, but the cost was high.

There were only three shades still fighting, if you

counted Giselle. At the same time, Alex wasn't convinced he was seeing everyone. They were too damned fast, and they knew how to use the shadows of the dental clinic to mask their movements further. And where the fuck was Hector?

He heard an anguished cry from Giselle, and looked back at her in time to see that she'd lost the machete thing in the fight. She stepped forward to hit Lindy, slowed down to human speed now, but Lindy stepped into the blow and, with a battle cry that chilled Alex's blood, swung her arm around hard enough to send the small dagger most of the way through Giselle's neck.

All around the room, the fighting faltered as Giselle's head flipped backward, held on by only a flap of skin. The body dropped to the ground.

Lindy stared down at it with red hooded eyes. Her clothes were torn and her hair was wild, blood dripping from the ends, and her face burning with terrible beauty. In that moment Alex felt like falling to her feet and begging for mercy. And she was on *their* side. She staggered, struggling to stay on her feet, until she stumbled far enough back to hit a wall.

With Giselle dead, the shades in the room began to step backward, and the BPI team advanced toward the patient rooms.

"ENOUGH."

The voice came from everywhere and nowhere. It seemed to suck all the air out of the room, draining Alex of what little energy he still felt. He fell to his knees—as did every single person, shade and human alike, in the room. Everyone except Lindy, who wheeled around and glowered at the man who'd just exited one of the patient rooms. Her arms hung frozen in the air with the push daggers dripping blood.

From head to toe he seemed like nothing special, just another thirtyish businessman in a nice suit. He carried no weapons at all, his hands loose at his sides. But his eyes were a red so dark they were nearly blue, and he radiated power and authority. He turned his head slowly, scowling around the room as though they were all kids who'd been playing music too loud. The shades all bowed their heads and murmured something that sounded like "my king."

"Don't worry," Lindy said to Alex, rolling her eyes. "He can only do that little trick once."

Alex staggered to his feet, the first one to manage to do so. Behind him, he heard several agents trying to crawl out the door. He didn't turn his head to look. "You must be Hector," he said in a voice that sounded much weaker than he'd intended. "Special Agent in Charge Alex McKenna. You're under arrest."

Hector didn't even glance his way. "You killed her," he

spat at Lindy. "She was my—"

"Your what? Pet psycho?" Lindy retorted, raising her weapons in a defensive position. "You didn't give a shit about her, any more than you do about Ambrose." Lindy hadn't lifted herself off the wall, and Alex suspected she was more hurt than she was letting on. Hector was looking at her as if lasers might shoot out of his eyes and fry her on the spot.

"Hey!" Alex interrupted, to break the spell between them. Both siblings looked over at him. Alex had the muzzle of his gun pointed squarely at Hector's heart. "You are under arrest," he said firmly, stepping toward Hector.

The shade just glared at him and looked back at his sister. "And what of your little friends here?" he asked. "Will you stand by and let him kill me? Or perhaps even help him?"

Lindy's posture sagged. With the blades by her sides, she said, "You have to answer for those kids, Hector. I won't kill you, but I won't stop Alex, either."

Hector's eyes gleamed. "*Alex,* huh?" He turned his attention to the BPI agent. "I do not recognize your government's sovereignty," he countered. "I am a king. And the stuff of nightmares."

The power in his voice sent a shock of fear up Alex's spine, but Lindy scoffed, limping forward to place herself between Hector and Alex. "You've been reading your own press again, brother," she said. "You are not the monster of fairy tales. You're just a man with a strange virus and an overinflated ego."

Hector's eyes narrowed. "You want a fairy tale?" he said very softly, taking a step forward. Alex couldn't see Lindy's face, but the fury on Hector's was enough to scare anyone. Alex inched a little bit to the right so he could shoot Hector without hitting Lindy. "I can give you a fairy tale," Hector taunted.

Before anyone could react, he blurred away from Lindy—straight at Alex.

~

To his credit, Alex McKenna got a shot off.

Unfortunately, it missed Hector entirely and buried itself in Lindy's right shoulder. She hissed with pain but still whirled around to follow Hector's progress. He charged at Alex, stepping into the agent's extended arm, and raised something—Giselle's blade, which he'd had hidden behind his back all along. Lindy saw him bring it down in a sweeping diagonal motion that sliced through the agent's cheek, chin, and straight down to the left subclavian artery in Alex's shoulder. Then Hector continued right on past him, straight for the exit that Giselle had opened up earlier.

Lindy screamed a curse and threw herself down beside Alex. Hector had cut deep; the wounds were spurting blood. The agent's good eye, the one that hadn't been filled with blood, stared up at her in confusion. More blood streamed down the side of his face and neck. Too much. She slapped her hand down over the artery to seal the wound, then realized that Hector had twisted the blade as it exited, making it nearly impossible to close the cut. "Fuck!"

He tried to say something, his lips twitching helplessly, but the effort made his cheeks move, and the pain was obvious. Lindy shook her head at him. "It's okay," she said, her own voice sounding high-pitched and uncertain. "You're gonna be okay." She tore her eyes away from him and looked up at the young female agent, Hadley, who was standing over them with wide eyes and clothes saturated in blood. More blood was splattered on her plastic visor, but she was still *standing,* and that was all Lindy cared about. "Call an ambulance," she snapped. "Do *not* pursue Hector. Take whatever shades you've arrested, zip tie the hell out of them, and keep them separated."

Hadley stared at her stupidly for a moment, swaying on her feet.

"*Do* it, Hadley," Lindy commanded, putting a little

force into her voice. Which made her sound like Hector. The young woman's eyes snapped into focus and then narrowed, but she scrambled away to follow Lindy's orders.

Lindy turned back to Alex. Arterial blood was still pumping out of his shoulder, running between her fingers. She fought against the desperate urge to dip her head down and drink it; shade saliva was an anti-coagulant, and she would only kill him faster. But she needed to get a lot of shade saliva into him quickly without letting it touch the main wound.

Then she got it. *I'll give you a fairy tale.* Oh, for heaven's sake.

Lindy bent her head down and kissed him.

At first she was just focused on getting saliva into his mouth, as gross as that sounded, but after a moment she felt something touch her face and she almost jumped. But it was him: He'd lifted the hand on his uninjured side to brush against her cheek. He began to return the kiss, tentatively at first, then with increasing enthusiasm. His lips were gentle, exploratory, and Lindy found herself getting caught up in it, to her own surprise. When was the last time she had kissed anyone like this? She could have mesmerized someone to make out with anytime she wanted, but that wasn't who Lindy wanted to be, and now she understood why. This was real. She could feel his attraction to her, like a pulse of electricity jolting across an invisible wire strung between them. She sent the same pulse back to him.

Behind her, a throat cleared impatiently. She got the impression it wasn't the first time. Embarrassed, Lindy sat up, her eyes going to the wound on Alex's shoulder. It was still bleeding, but in a sluggish trail now. The artery had sealed back up. She sighed in relief and turned around to see a slightly amused paramedic. "Okay if we take him now, ma'am?"

Lindy nodded, rising to make room. Alex's eyes followed her. As she stepped back she glanced down at her own wound, from the bullet in her shoulder. Some of Alex's blood had gotten into her mouth, helping her heal, but it was still bleeding. In fact . . . Lindy frowned down at her shirt and then looked at Alex as the paramedics strapped him to the stretcher, comparing the bloodstains. Had her blood gotten into his wound? That didn't—

"Ms. Frederick?" The voice was Hadley's, and although Lindy was pretty sure she'd asked the young agent to call her by her first name, the blank, professional look on her face suggested she wouldn't be coming over to braid Lindy's hair anytime soon. Hadley gestured to the prone figure behind her, whom the paramedics were working on. "Agent Wu is dying," she said matter-offactly. This was one of the agents whom the shades had practically drained. "Is there anything you can do? To heal her, I mean," she rushed to add, in case Lindy had thought she was asking her to transmute the agent. That, Lindy would not do.

"Yeah, I'm coming." She went over to the paramedics to borrow a syringe. No more kissing.

~

Alex McKenna was sent into surgery, and the dental clinic was swarmed by local cops, FBI bureaucrats, and the media. Chase Eddy had driven down to take charge of the scene. He vouched for her, guided her through making a statement, and made sure that everyone left out any mention of Lindy's status. It looked as if her condition would remain a BPI secret—at least for now.

In the end, seven of the eight remaining teens were rescued and sent home to their families. They were traumatized and shaken, with armfuls of puncture marks, but in good physical condition: Hector had wanted them healthy for the experiments.

The body of the eighth teenager was never found, and Lindy suspected that the kid Giselle had drained was not dead, but transmuted now, and had been taken away with the rest of Hector's people.

Alex's team had lost seven agents, one for each of the lives they'd saved. Three of Hector's shades surrendered and were shipped east to Camp Vamp in armored cars, covered in zip ties. The rest of them either had escaped or were killed. Although Lindy had spotted at least twelve dead shades, curiously, not a single shade corpse was found on-site—they'd been removed by the other shades in the chaos, but Lindy saw more than one newspaper that suggested they'd turned to ash. She knew that Hector was trying to keep the human authorities from having a body to autopsy, and if it fueled the vampire legend, well, all the better.

When Chase Eddy finally sent her back to the hotel at 9 a.m., Lindy went straight to the hotel restaurant and enticed a jet-legged stranger up to her room for a feeding. She sent him away a little light-headed and convinced he'd had the best sex of his life, which was a pretty big win for someone who was drinking mimosas alone in a hotel restaurant at nine in the morning.

That afternoon Lindy went to see Alex McKenna at the hospital. She had showered, rested, and fed again, and his good eye brightened when she walked into the room. The other eye was covered by the same bandage that swathed his cheek, shoulder, and chin.

"Hi," she said, feeling a little awkward.

"Hey, Lindy." The words came out a tiny bit slurred,

dropping the *d* in Lindy's name, and she figured the clear liquid in his IV was probably morphine.

"Hey." She looked over at the FBI agent seated in the corner of his room. The man had taken possession of Alex's remote and was flipping through the channels. "Can you give us a minute?" The guard looked at Alex, who held up a weak thumb. The guard shrugged, turned off the TV, and left the room, mumbling something about ESPN.

Ignoring him, Alex looked at Lindy. The visible corner of his mouth crooked up. "We did it."

"Well, sort of." She sat down in the visitor chair next to his bed. "Hector got away. *I* let him get away." She heard the guilt in her own voice, and she couldn't meet Alex's eyes.

"To save me," he reminded her. "And we got the kids home. And Giselle is dead."

Lindy couldn't help but smile at that. "You should have seen Ruiz's face when Agent Eddy told him about that," she told Alex. "He hasn't forgiven me for being a shade, but for a second there I thought he was going to actually hug me."

Alex's smile widened, until he winced with pain. "Ooh. Don't be funny."

"I promise nothing." She hesitated a moment, looking over the machines that were currently hooked up to Alex

McKenna. Had it been worth it? The fledgling BPI had lost so much. They'd rescued the teenagers, yes, and it was true that they'd put a serious crimp in Hector's operation by killing his lackeys. Especially Giselle. She had wanted to kill that bitch for years, and Lindy had to admit it'd felt great.

But now Hector would go underground and begin building his army back up again—this time with her blood to help him experiment. When she had time to think about it, she'd realized that was what he'd been doing during the beginning of the fight—making sure Stella and the blood samples were safe.

He had to be stopped, and Lindy was the only one strong enough to do it. If the BPI was going to let her do that, great. If not, though, she'd have to get rid of the bracelet and go after him herself.

Meanwhile, if the morning news was any indication, the bloodbath at the dental clinic had woken the sleeping giant of public opinion. A few weeks ago they'd been happy to ignore "the shade issue," as though Lindy's kind was just a flu outbreak in a couple of counties, but today every headline in the country screamed the word *Vampires*. Lindy had no idea what it would mean for her or for the BPI, but change was in the air. She didn't like being unsure of her footing.

It wasn't the right moment to say any of that, though.

"You're going to have a pretty great scar, huh?" she teased him. "I hear chicks dig the scars."

The corner of his mouth turned up, but fatigue was creeping over his pale face. "Oh yeah. That's me. All about the chicks." She smiled. "You know," he added drowsily, "you're a pretty good kisser."

Lindy stood up. "And that's my cue." She went over and pecked his exposed cheek, being very chaste about it. "Get better, Alex. I think the BPI is going to need you." *I'm going to need you,* she added silently.

She was almost at the door when his sleepy voice followed her. "I need you, too," he murmured.

Lindy froze. She turned around to face him. "What did you say?"

Epilogue

Special Agent Chase Eddy didn't make it back to the hotel until late afternoon. It had been a rough twelve hours of handling the criminologists and the media and Alex's supervisors, including a very worried Deputy Director Harding. Chase had to spend forty minutes on a conference call with her and Alex's surgeon before she agreed that she didn't need to rush out there.

In the hotel elevator, he leaned his head against the cool metal wall, his body coming down from all the caffeine and adrenaline. He'd been Alex's second in command for years, and the two of them could switch roles if the situation required it, but that didn't make it easy. There would still be plenty of repercussions, he knew, but the immediate crisis was finally winding down enough for him to take a well-earned nap.

Chase staggered down the hall to his door, yawning the whole way. He fumbled out his key card and managed to open the door on the third try. He really *was* tired.

Inside the hotel room, he flipped on the lights and pulled his wallet and keys out of his pockets, setting them down on the counter that stood outside the little bathroom door. He set his service weapon there, too, and continued into the room feeling much lighter. He wondered if he should jump in the shower now or just collapse for a few—

"Hello."

Chase jumped. The voice had come from a man leaning against the wall he'd just walked past. He was a blond Caucasian man of about thirty, wearing a rumpled-looking suit, and for a second Chase thought the hotel had put another agent in his room by mistake. Weirder things had happened at these mid-level chain hotels. "Hi," he said uncertainly. "Um, who are you?"

The other man gave him a jovial smile. "I'm Hector," he replied. "And I'm here to make you an offer."

Acknowledgments

I had a blast working on *Nightshades,* and that never would have been possible without the help of a few wonderful people. Thank you to my husband, who put up with my feverish writing habits, and to my brother-in-law Kraig for the weird drug advice ("Can we talk about meth? Is this a good time?") I have so much gratitude for my entire Olson and Harms families, who never actually said, "Really, vampires again?" even though they were probably thinking it. They advocate for all my books despite the genre being way outside their comfort zones, and if I didn't already love them so much I'd love them just for that. Hashtag blessed.

Thank you to Mark Teppo for the beta read and confidence boost right when I really needed both, and to the team at Tor.com who produced such a great cover and thoughtful edit. My thanks especially to Lee Harris for believing in me—and also for erasing that video from karaoke like he promised he would.

And this wouldn't be complete without me thanking the Old World readers who followed my work to *Nightshades.* I know this is a little different, but I really hope you had a great time with the BPI gang. Or at least a good time. Or a medium-okay time. But seriously, thank you.

About the Author

Melissa Olson was born and raised in Chippewa Falls, Wisconsin, and studied film and literature at the University of Southern California in Los Angeles. After graduation, and a brief stint bouncing around the Hollywood studio system, Melissa landed in Madison, Wisconsin, where she eventually acquired a master's degree from UW-Milwaukee, a husband, a mortgage, two kids, and two comically oversized dogs, not at all in that order. She loves Madison, but still dreams of the food in LA. Literally. There are dreams. Learn more about Melissa, her work, and her dog at www.MelissaFOlson.com.

TOR·COM

Science fiction. Fantasy. The universe.

And related subjects.

*

More than just a publisher's website, *Tor.com* is a venue for **original fiction, comics,** and **discussion** of the entire field of SF and fantasy, in all media and from all sources. Visit our site today—and join the conversation yourself.